BRANDON'S EMPIRE

Also by L.P. Holmes
in Large Print:

Flame of Sunset

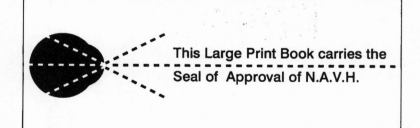

This Large Print Book carries the
Seal of Approval of N.A.V.H.

BRANDON'S EMPIRE

L.P. HOLMES

Thorndike Press • Thorndike, Maine

Published in 1997 by arrangement with Golden West
Literary Agency.

Thorndike Large Print ® Western Series.

The tree indicium is a trademark of Thorndike Press.

The text of this Large Print edition is unabridged.
Other aspects of the book may vary from the original edition.

Set in 16 pt. Plantin by Warren S. Doersam.

Printed in the United States on permanent paper.

Libarary of Congress Cataloging in Publication Data

Holmes, L.P. (Llewellyn Perry), 1895–
    Brandon's empire / L.P. Holmes.
      p.   cm.
    ISBN 0-7862-1196-2 (lg. print : hc : alk. paper)
    1. Large type books. I. Title.
[PS3515.O4448B7   1997]
  813′.54—dc21
                                                       97-36733

BRANDON'S EMPIRE

CHAPTER ONE

It was mid-afternoon when Leach Carlin, a pair of pack horses at lead behind him, rode out of the shadowed mouth of Fandango Canyon into the first long flatness of Big Sage Prairie. Here the late September sun struck with solid heat in air so still that little bombs of dust punched up by the hoofs of the horses rose scarcely more than fetlock high before settling back to the thick, muffling silence of the stage road.

Once free of the winding confines of the canyon, the road ran arrow straight through the sage for a long mile before losing itself among the spread of buildings and rows of tapered green lombardy poplar trees that was Modoc City. Way out east of town, far across the prairie's empty distance, the Nevada Hills angled strongly up, their tawny flanks daubed and speckled with the scattered dark touch of juniper and cedar and mahogany thickets.

This morning, in a lofty park of the Warner Mountains, Carlin had awakened under blankets stiff with frost. Up there the aspens were already taking on shadings of gold, the cherry brush was showing a blush of crimson, and the curving timber benches lay lost and drowsing and still in the blue and smoky veils of autumn haze. After four unbroken months in the high parks where the air was crisp and keen, Carlin now stirred in his saddle in unconscious protest against this sultry breath of a lower country.

Those months in the Warners had left their mark on Carlin. He was ragged and shaggy and Indian dark from wind and sun; and whisker stubble shadowed and roughened his jaws and cheeks. In the saddle he shaped up as a rangy, flat-backed figure of a man, long of leg, taut and compact about the hips, with much of his weight in the strong arch of his chest and the solid width of his shoulders. His cheek bones were high, giving a cast of angularity to his features; and his eyes, squinting a little against the sun glare, were a cool blue, though touched just now with a certain skeptical reticence that was only a shade away from bitterness as his glance ran ahead to take in the familiar outlines of the town.

Man, he mused, was a homing animal. No matter how many disillusioning disappointments he might have experienced on it, once he had marked a land with his toil and watered it with his sweat, he knew a certain eagerness on coming back to it.

The horses, sensing the end of a journey, speeded up their jog and swiftly cut down the interval of distance. Here, halfway along Bidwell Street, the stage road came in at a direct right angle, and at this corner Carlin turned left and pulled up in front of Billy Prior's store. For a moment he stayed in his saddle, while his glance touched all the well-remembered length of the street, and it struck him that the town seemed strangely empty and silent, almost as though brooding over something.

He put this thought aside, swung down, ducked under the hitch rail and dragged his spurs across the porch and through the store's open, shadowy doorway. Here again were familiar surroundings — the spreading, warm gloom, the stacks and rows and shelves of varied merchandise, mingled odors of dry-goods and hardware, of bacon and coffee and the penetrating spice of dried onions.

The store, like the town, was empty and silent, but Carlin, knowing his way around in here, went on back past the far end of the counter, thumped a fist against a door there and lifted his voice.

"Billy! Oh — Billy!"

The answer carried a growl of exasperation. "You'll have to wait until I finish getting dressed." The words ran off in a low mutter of profanity.

The shadow of a smile touched Carlin's lips as he opened the door and stepped through into Billy Prior's living quarters. The storekeeper was a rotund little man, with a ruddy, cherubic face. He was in his underwear, sitting on the edge of his bed, pulling on his socks. At Carlin's abrupt entrance a growl of anger started in his throat, then ran out into an exclamation of pure pleasure.

"Leach! Be damned! Man, you startled me."

Carlin's smile widened as he looked down at this old friend. "Something new, isn't it, Billy? You getting all spruced up in the middle of the afternoon. What's the occasion? Now don't tell me that at your age —"

"Funeral, Leach," cut in Billy. "Dan Brandon's funeral."

Carlin's smile was abruptly gone. "Dan Brandon!"

The storekeeper bobbed his head. "That's it. Dan Brandon. Five o'clock or thereabouts this afternoon. Dan died day before yesterday."

Carlin let out a long, slow breath. "Natural causes?"

Billy Prior nodded again. "You know how old Dan was. Always on the hussle and too cussed stubborn to admit his years or the fact that all men are bound to grow old. Doc Persall warned him a couple of months ago, but Dan wouldn't listen. So-o!" The little storekeeper shrugged, then added, "And Dan, being the kind of man he was, had his enemies. Mike Quarney never let up hating him. Case Broderick has done his share of snorting and stamping and pawing the dust. Then there's the small fry, like Shep Bowen and Vern DeLong, hanging around like a pair of coyotes, waiting their chance to take a bite out of the old bull's hide. On top of all the rest, there's been Clint."

"Yeah," murmured Carlin. "There's always Clint. What's he been doing now?"

"Bungling ranch affairs, plenty — from all I hear. I think, more than any other one thing, that old Dan's disappointment in his son is what really pulled him down. Dan had a lot of big plans built around Clint, and he didn't give up hope for a long time. I guess he finally had to admit that it just wasn't any use, and that broke his heart. Anyhow, Dan Brandon's dead and is being buried this afternoon and I'm one of the pallbearers. A chore I don't care for, but one I couldn't rightly refuse when Mrs. Brandon sent word through Doc Persall, asking me."

"No," agreed Carlin slowly, "you couldn't." He thumbed his pockets for tobacco and papers, came up with Durham sack empty to limpness, then spied a full sack on Billy Prior's bureau and helped himself to that. He was somberly silent until a thin haze of blue smoke curled up before his face.

"This is a jolt to me, Billy. I can think of a lot of people I'd rather see buried than Dan Brandon."

Billy Prior tipped his head, gave Carlin a short keen glance.

"And I can think of a lot who wouldn't be as charitable as you right now, Leach. Old Dan didn't give you the best deal in the world."

"Clint's fault," said Carlin quietly. "Dan was just taking his son's part. And any father can be excused for that. It was the only blind spot Dan Brandon had, his belief in Clint. Outside of that he was the biggest man I've ever known. And he built the best damn ranch I ever saw. He was a tall oak, Billy."

The storekeeper pulled on his pants and reached for a shoe. "He was that, and he'll be missed — plenty! But have a thought,

12

Leach, where the real tragedy of this thing comes in. Dan's gone, and his troubles done with. But for Martha Brandon, they're just beginning. She put in her life helping Dan build up Hackamore. Now she'll have to sit and watch the ranch fall apart, because Quarney and Broderick and the others will really go to work on it, now. Clint will never stand up to those fellows like old Dan did. He'll show as a damned weak crutch for Martha Brandon to lean on in her old age. Yes sir — that's the tough part of the picture."

The storekeeper pulled on his other shoe, laced it and stood up, reaching for his shirt. Then he switched the subject.

"How'd you make out up in the Warners — any luck at all?"

Carlin reached inside his shirt, brought out a sweat-stained well-padded buckskin money belt and tossed it on the bed.

"There it is, Billy. Twenty-eight hundred dollars. I combed every gulch and aspen swamp from Hardin Peak to Big Dismal. I rooted out an even hundred and forty head carrying Pete Jacobsen's Par Seven iron. I put them across the pass on to Mack Shaw's range and Mack took them all at a straight twenty dollars a head."

Billy Prior gave a small exclamation of

pleasure. "Now that's a lot better than I expected. Made things really worth-while for both of us. Split the money down the middle, Leach."

"Oh, no," protested Carlin. "You're being too damn generous. I've no legitimate right to half."

"Hell you haven't!" barked the storekeeper. "That was our agreement, wasn't it — half and half? It sure was. You were playing just as big a gamble as I was. You didn't know whether you'd find one or a dozen head of Jacobsen's old herd up there. I loaned Pete a thousand dollars against those cattle. If Pete had lived, the best I'd done was get back my thousand and maybe a little interest. This way I'm more than to the good. I'm satisfied. So, you're taking a full half and not one cent less. By the look of you, you worked plenty hard to earn it."

Carlin scrubbed a big, callused palm across his bristly jaw. "I'm pretty frowsy, for a fact. I could sure use your water and tub, some new clothes off your shelves, and then a haircut and shave at Andy Foote's."

"Fly to it. Help yourself to what you want. By the way, did you run across any sign of others being interested in the Jacobsen herd?"

Carlin smiled faintly. "Some. Met up with

14

Shep Bowen and Vern DeLong one day. They had eight or ten head bunched in a little park and were all thumbs and left feet when I rode in on them. I thanked them for making the gather, and then suggested the shortest trail back to Big Sage Prairie. They took it. Another day, just south of Big Dismal, it was Case Broderick and Duff Randall. They weren't exactly friendly. When I asked Broderick if Pete Jacobsen had ever owed him any more, they took the hint and cleared out, too."

"Wouldn't trust any of them from here to you," snorted Billy Prior. "For all his strut and swagger, Case Broderick has all the instincts of a thief. Better stoke the stove up, Leach, if you want that hot water."

Late afternoon shadows laid a cooling pattern along the street. Over in front of the church the funeral cortege was forming. The old hearse, which Coony Fyle had brought from his livery barn, stood directly in front of the church door. Coony had done the best he could to spruce up the old vehicle and the team which drew it. Now, plainly uncomfortable in a rusty suit of black store clothes, Coony stood waiting, looking even more the undertaker than did Doc Persall, who was talking to him.

The church itself was a sturdy little building, with the lift of a modest, square-sided steeple to mark its small, quiet dignity. This, along with a coat of white paint which the prairie sun had not as yet had time to fade and dull, made the little edifice stand out in staunch contrast to the weathered, neutral shades of the balance of the buildings in this town of Modoc City.

For the past half hour, people had been drifting into town. In line behind the hearse were several buckboards and spring wagons, empty now, their owners assembled in the church. A scattering of saddle broncs stood at various hitch rails along the street, dozing hip-shot, or stamping and switching at flies. On the porch of Pee Dee Kyne's Prairie House Hotel, the lank figure of Mike Quarney was hunched in a chair, the smoke of a cigar wreathing his angular face. In the shade of the overhang of Billy Prior's store, several men lounged.

Stepping out of the barber shop, Leach Carlin paused to let his glance take in the run of the street again. The kiss of Andy Foote's razor had put a smooth, bronze shine across the flat planes of Carlin's lean cheeks and brought out more sharply the solid line of his jaw. An all-over feeling of physical fitness lay in him, but his thoughts still held in a somber vein.

He was thinking of Hackamore. The ranch of a man's dreams. Once so strong and powerful but now, according to what Billy Prior had said, beginning to shake apart. Because a strong man had died and there was no one of like strength to take his place. Carlin shook his head. So much for a man's lifetime of toil.

Carlin's glance touched the figure of Mike Quarney on the hotel porch, then swung to the group in front of the store. Among others there he saw Duff Randall and Shep Bowen and Vern DeLong. A little gust of bleakness twisted Carlin's lips.

They've been waiting a long time for this, he thought. And now that it's happened, they're here to gloat.

He broke a fresh sack of Durham from his shirt pocket, twisted up a smoke, then moved with slow and casual ease toward the store. Young Jimmy Spurlock was there, as was grizzled Joe Spence. A little apart from the rest stood lank, thin-faced Hitch Wheeler, a gaunt shoulder point propped against the building. He swung his head as Carlin passed him, nodded, but said nothing.

Feeling the weight of Carlin's steady survey, Duff Randall and Shep Bowen gave it back to him, Randall with his usual heavy-lipped, challenging mockery, while Shep Bowen showed a sly, calculating half smile, Vern DeLong, a half-breed, sucked on a cigarette, stared straight ahead. Crusty Joe Spence spoke up.

"Cowboy, I thought this country had lost you."

Jimmy Spurlock, hunkered on his heels beside the stove door, lifted a greeting hand.

"Leach! You've been gone too long. The word bring you to town?"

Carlin shook his head as he eased down beside the young rider. "Didn't know a thing about it until Billy Prior told me, an hour or so ago."

Young Jimmy's voice ran sober. "I just can't seem to get used to it being a fact. Old Dan always seemed too solid to die. Like a rock that had always been there and always would be there. Now that he's gone, I got a damned uncomfortable feeling that this prairie is pretty empty."

Duff Randall flipped a dead cigarette butt into the street's dust, spat after it, and spoke with heavy, cynical sarcasm.

"Nothing makes me so sick as to listen to a lot of mealy-mouthed talk about a man after he's dead. If he was a damned high-and-mighty old buzzard while he was alive

18

— which Dan Brandon sure enough was — then by dying he don't turn into any saint. Wipe your nose, Spurlock — and grow up!"

At Randall's side, Shep Bowen laughed thinly. "Don't worry about the prairie being empty, Spurlock. It'll manage to get along without Dan Brandon around, trying to run everything and everybody. Damned if I can get your point. Brandon fired you, didn't he, not over a week or so before he died?"

"Could have been my own fault," retorted Jimmy. "Besides, at that time he was already a sick man."

Bowen laughed again, scoffingly. "Why make allowances for him? He never made 'em for anybody else."

"Hackamore was Dan Brandon's life," defended Jimmy. "And he saw to the running of it, his way. That was his right."

Duff Randall spat again. "He saw to a lot of things, all his way. Even to staking that church to a new coat of paint. He must have known he was about done for and he wanted the church bright and pretty for his last trip through it. That was Dan Brandon for you. Stepping high, wide and handsome, even on his way to hell."

There was a short moment of uneasy silence, then Jimmy Spurlock, badgered into anger, started to push to his feet. Leach Carlin dropped a restraining hand on the kid's arm and pulled him back.

"Easy, kid. There'll always be those loose in the tongue about a man — after he's dead."

Duff Randall came around, his neck swelling, his broad, heavy face swept with a quick tide of anger. He was a burly one, this Randall, heavy-legged and with a long, thick body.

"I say what I please, when I please, Carlin."

Carlin's drawl was far softer than his glance. "Don't take a lick of nerve to curse a dead man, Randall."

The growling anger in Randall deepened, then quieted as Shep Bowen said, "Here comes Case."

Case Broderick came in at the south end of town, riding at a lope. He pulled up in the middle of the street and sat staring at the funeral cortege. Joe Spence shuffled his boots and spoke dryly.

"Get ready to bark and roll over, Randall. Yonder's your master."

Duff Randall came back harshly. "Soften it down, Spence. Nobody asked for your opinion."

Spence surveyed Randall bleakly out of sun-and-wind-puckered eyes. "But I gave it.

Don't yap at me. I'm too old to fool, too old to scare. Hell with you!"

Case Broderick swung his black horse over to the store hitch rail. He jerked a short nod toward the church.

"So he's common clay, after all. A lot of fools can now wonder why they used to bow and scrape so low and humble in front of him."

Duff Randall used his heavy sarcasm again. "Better watch yourself, Case. Carlin here is taking exception to any kind of free speech."

Broderick stepped from his saddle, a solid, big-boned man, with a thin-lipped, ungenerous mouth. His eyes, deep-set, were chill gimlets. There was no charity or softness in this man anywhere. He touched Carlin swiftly with a slanting glance.

"So! I can't imagine why."

Carlin met the look with a casual indifference. "Does it matter? And if so, what about it?"

Before Broderick could answer, the store door opened and Billy Prior came out, locking the door behind him. Billy was dressed in his somber best for a somber occasion. Case Broderick, flushing slightly from the careless challenge in Carlin's words, blocked the little storekeeper's way.

21

"You can't lock up now, Prior. Some things I want. Open up again."

Billy shook his head. "Not now. Store's closed for a couple of hours. Come around then."

"No!" insisted Broderick. "Not then — now! Now's when I want to spend my money. Besides, you're not going anywhere in particular."

Billy Prior stared up at Broderick, then spoke stoutly. "That's where you're wrong. I'm going to pay my last respects to an old friend. You heard what I said. The store is closed until after the funeral."

He pushed past Broderick and started to step off the low porch to the street. It was Duff Randall who stuck out a treacherous, tripping foot. Billy Prior staggered, fought to keep his balance, then pitched forward into the street's dust on his hands and knees. Randall grinned mockingly.

"Prior, you're getting fat and clumsy."

The storekeeper got back to his feet. One knee of his trousers was split. He dusted himself off and looked at Randall, eyes bright with anger. He spoke with a low distinctness.

"Randall, you're a dirty dog!"

With that he turned and went on across the street. Randall reared up, made as if to go after him, but stopped when Leach Carlin's voice hit out.

"That's far enough, Randall. Stay right there!"

As he spoke, Carlin came to his feet and moved forward. "Billy called you by your right name, Randall. Now, I'm going across the street. Maybe you'd like to try and trip me. If so, have at it!"

Grizzled, tough old Joe Spence put in a cutting drawl. "He won't, Leach. You're more his size and you're looking at him."

Duff Randall spun around to face Carlin, his head dropping low and forward between his burly shoulders. His fists were balled and his knees slightly sprung. He looked like a bear, ready to charge. Then it was Hitch Wheeler, until this moment a silently lounging figure in the background, who put in his first word.

"Easy, men — easy! This is a solemn occasion and no time to start a ruckus. Wouldn't be seemly."

He was lank and shadow-thin, this Hitch Wheeler, with bleached hair and a narrow, sardonic face which seemed at all times to reflect a cynical recklessness and some thread of a secret inner amusement, as though he found the world and all men in it something to disbelieve and jeer at.

Across Big Sage Prairie his reputation was checkered and no man was entirely sure just how much of this reputation was fact and how much was fancy. He never held a steady job, yet he never seemed to lack for money in his pocket. He was a lone wolf of a man who gave off the impression of being completely without fear and possessed of an element of danger bleak enough to give any man pause. So it was that his drawled words now brought about an arresting moment of quiet.

In this moment of trenchant silence, a surrey came rolling into town. Driving the slow-pacing team was Clint Brandon, his face dark and smooth under a tall, white Stetson. On the seat beside him was Sam Desmond, his bluster for once stilled. The back seat held two women, both dressed in black. There was Beth Desmond, her full, sultry young beauty in no way dimmed by the somber attire she wore. With her was Martha Brandon, Dan's widow. Behind the surrey, riding two and two, came the six members of the Hackamore crew.

Leach Carlin had always thought Martha Brandon one of the most remarkable women he'd ever known. Against her black mourning attire her hair looked snowy, and the grief that was most certainly hers was hidden deep within her. Her head was high, her face composed in unflinching dignity.

With a gesture purely instinct, Leach Carlin took off his hat and beside him, Joe Spence and Jimmy Spurlock did the same. Then it was Hitch Wheeler's voice again, soft as a summer wind, drifting along the length of the store porch.

"Now there's an idea, Carlin — and all to your credit. For once we'll all be gentlemen. All right, Broderick and the rest of you, hats off! For you're looking at a great lady."

Shep Bowen and Vern DeLong, startled, moved to obey. But Case Broderick and Duff Randall paid no attention. So Hitch Wheeler spoke again and while his voice was still low, it now carried a wicked ring.

"God damn it — I said hats off!"

Broderick and Randall swung their heads toward Wheeler, angry disbelief in their eyes.

"Yeah," murmured Wheeler. "I said it and I meant it. Get 'em off!"

A hint of that faint, sardonic smile touched Wheeler's lips again, but what Broderick and Randall saw behind that smile made up their minds for them. They took off their hats, Randall with a surly fuming, Broderick with no other expression beyond a pinching down of his cold eyes.

The surrey pulled in ahead of the hearse and the occupants stepped down, Doc Persall giving an aiding hand to the two women. Before moving on into the church, Martha Brandon glanced at the men across the street. She inclined her head slightly, then went on in on Doc Persall's arm. Beth Desmond and Clint Brandon followed, with Sam Desmond and the Hackamore crew bringing up the rear.

Carlin stepped out into the street, Joe Spence and Jimmy Spurlock beside him. Carlin swung his head and caught Hitch Wheeler's eye. Wheeler shook his head.

"Not me, Carlin. Was I to go in there, then Dan Brandon wouldn't rest easy. More than once he said he hoped to see the day when I'd be hung. No point in mocking a dead man."

When Carlin and his two companions disappeared through the church door, Case Broderick turned to Hitch Wheeler, his voice running harsh.

"You threw your weight around just now, Wheeler. You got away with it because the situation happened to be as it was. But don't get too proud about it!"

Wheeler met Broderick's cold stare with open insolence. "Well?" he murmured.

They looked their badgered anger at him,

but as before there was that hint of dismal chill behind Wheeler's twisted grin to give them pause. Wheeler tipped his narrow head slightly.

"That's being smart, gentlemen. Always remember it. So far — and no further!"

He backed away past the corner of the store, then turned and went off down street. He turned into Ace Lanier's Skyhigh bar, reappeared shortly after, got his horse and jogged leisurely out of town. Duff Randall glared heavy anger after him.

"Some across this prairie are going to learn the hard way, Case."

Broderick shrugged. "They'll learn."

In the church the services were mercifully brief. This was a country of brevity in such things. Words were superfluous. It was how men felt in the deep springs of their beings that counted. All present had known Dan Brandon's faults as well as his virtues. Most of them had, at one time or another, quarreled with him. Some had even felt that they hated him. Yet not one of them, in these brief moments of honest reflection, but had to admit he respected the dead man. And so, here in the humble little square-sided church, they now gave of that respect to the memory of a man who had left a definite imprint on a tough land and across the lives of other men.

The pallbearers were Bois Renfro, Sam Desmond, Buell Hadley, and Billy Prior.

Leach Carlin did not follow the cortege out to the little cemetery southwest of town. Instead, along with Joe Spence and Jimmy Spurlock, he drifted down street to the Sky-high. Duff Randall, Shep Bowen, and Vern DeLong were there, among others, drinks in front of them at the far end of the bar. Carlin rang a coin on the bar and Ace Lanier slid bottle and glasses over. Carlin poured for his companions and himself.

"When he fired me because I wouldn't stand for any more of Clint's damned, sneaky rawhiding, I figured I was set to hate Dan Brandon forever," remarked Joe Spence soberly. "Now I find that I don't. I find myself remembering him at the times when he stood big and threw a long shadow."

"That's it, Joe," nodded Jimmy Spurlock — "that's it. Old Dan had a sort of queer twist about Clint, but past that he was plenty of man. Here's to him!"

Leach Carlin lifted his glass. "Right!"

They touched their glasses and drank. From his spot, Duff Randall spoke roughly.

"Makes me sicker by the minute. I still say he was an old bastard, and I hope the gates of hell are reaching for him right now!"

As he spoke, Randall came along in front of the bar with his rolling, heavy-legged swagger. He had several drinks in him and being the sort that liquor set fire to, was showing the stirred-up brutality that was always crouched and eager in him. He stopped; doubled fists on his hips, looking Carlin up and down. He spoke again with his heavy jeering.

"Still feeling proud, maybe? Still aiming to tell other men what they can or can't say?"

Carlin, impassive of face, looked this crass and burly fellow over. Then he nodded, as though come to some inevitable decision. He put his glass back on the bar and spoke evenly.

"There comes a time, Randall. There always comes a time!"

He pivoted slightly and drove a knotted fist into Duff Randall's face.

CHAPTER TWO

The blow hung Randall on his heels and held him floundering for a moment. Carlin, now that he had committed himself to this thing, went in fast and whipped home two more slashing punches, one of which brought a gout of crimson from Randall's lips, the other biting into the side of his neck, under the ear.

An average man might have been floored then and there, but not Duff Randall. Animal stamina lay deep in this thick-bodied fellow, and though Carlin's last blow swung him against the bar Randall bounced off and came in with a low, driving lunge which put his shoulder into Carlin's chest and enabled him to get his arms around Carlin in a bear hug.

For a moment Randall seemed content with this, while he got his jarred senses straightened out. At the far end of the bar Shep Bowen and Vern DeLong traded swift and meaning glances and came moving up. Joe Spence slapped an open hand on the bar with sharp, explosive impact. It jerked the

30

attention of Bowen and DeLong to him and Joe spoke with a flat emphasis.

"Stay there! No ganging up. Randall asked for this, and he's going to get it. Stay where you are!"

They marked the bleakness in Joe's eyes and came no closer.

As Randall's bear hug set down, Leach Carlin stiffened his spine against the pressure and with both arms free, hooked short, down-curving blows at the back of Randall's neck and the base of his skull. The rabbit punches stirred Randall to a burst of action. He spread his thick legs and began driving Carlin back with short, plunging jumps, trying to pin him solidly against something.

Carlin gave way until they had moved well clear of the bar, then braced his right side against Randall's drive, which made Randall swing round and round in a circle that got him nowhere. Their plunging, trampling course carried them over beside a poker table where Randall got tangled up in a chair and partially tripped. Trying to get his feet solidly under him again, Randall loosened his hold slightly and Carlin jerked free. Then Randall threw a clubbing, round-house swing which thudded against the top of Carlin's shoulder, bounced off and skidded a heavy fist across his face.

The blow, partially deflected though it was, shook Carlin up and brought the ooze of blood across his lips. Randall seized on this advantage with a whine of eagerness and came driving in, hammering a sledging fist into the center of Carlin's chest. The punch hurt Carlin all the way through, drove the breath from him and sent him reeling back.

It did something else to him. Up until now, he'd gone at this affair with the cold, calculating purpose of knocking some of the swaggering ego out of Randall. But the taste of his own blood across his lips and the aching numbness which now filled his chest loosed a sudden black, destroying savagery in him. His bloodied lips pulled thin and merciless and the blue of his eyes turned dark.

He measured Randall as the latter came surging in once more, ducked under a clubbing fist, sighted for his adversary's throat and drove the blow home wickedly.

It was brutal; it was crippling, deliberately aimed and landed. It did what it was calculated to do. Randall fell back, gagging and choking, hands pawing at his paralyzed throat. Carlin, savage and unrelenting now, crowded him, smashing both fists to Randall's sagging and unprotected jaw. Randall floundered against the bar, grabbing at it for support. That blow to the throat had taken all the fight out of him. His eyes were wild and staring and he strangled thickly for air.

There was no pity in Carlin. He hauled his man away from the bar's support and hammered him again and again on the jaw. Randall's eyes dulled and he began to sag, finally dropping to his knees, where he hunkered, hugging his face and head with his arms. His fight for air was a hoarse, thickly shuddering gasping.

Carlin stepped back, watched his man for a moment, then leaned over and scooped up his hat, which he'd lost in the first fury of Randall's charge. Carlin was panting heavily himself and his chest still felt as though the kick of a horse had landed there. He scrubbed the back of a hand across his bleeding lips and his words ran rough as he looked at Shep Bowen and the swarthy-faced Vern DeLong.

"He's your friend, it seems. You can have him now. And when he's able to talk again, maybe he'll watch his damned nasty tongue."

Carlin turned and went out, followed silently by Joe Spence and Jimmy Spurlock. He led the way back to Billy Prior's store and settled down there on the porch. He got out his smoking and fumbled a cigarette into shape, his hands feeling stiff and clumsy. The smoke bit and stung his lacerated lips, and after the first drag he threw the cigarette into the street. Joe Spence gave out with his dry, slightly nasal drawl.

"Barely possible that jigger will be easier to live with, now."

Jimmy Spurlock, young enough to be a trifle awed by the burst of violence he'd just witnessed, blurted, "He asked for it. He was bound to force trouble."

"Feeling his oats," said Joe Spence. "Be quite a few that way, now that Dan Brandon's dead and gone."

Carlin brooded, saying nothing. The embers of that sudden gust of black fury were now beginning to cool a little, leaving him as such an affair always did, low and depressed in his mind. The reaction was always thus. The dregs of anything, he mused bleakly, were always bitter and rough across a man's tongue.

On the porch of the Prairie House, Mike Quarney still sat, smoking. He had watched the funeral pass with no other sign than a mocking glitter in his eyes. After that he'd been joined by Case Broderick and they had traded comment back and forth in low tones. Now Broderick left his chair, stood for a moment at the edge of the porch, a cigar clipped at an upward angle in his teeth as he looked along the street. Then he moved down, came along and turned into the Sky-high.

He was in there for only a little time before coming into view again, anger showing in the swing of his shoulders. The glance he sent across at the store and the men waiting in front of it, was dark and sharp. Shep Bowen and Vern DeLong came out of the Skyhigh, followed by Duff Randall.

Randall was still none too steady on his feet and his head sagged between hunched and heavy shoulders. Broderick turned to the three of them and there was an exchange of words, with Broderick doing most of the talking, emphasizing what he had to say with a hard swing of his hand. After which the three sought their horses and rode out of town. Broderick went back to the hotel.

The funeral was over and done with. Dan Brandon was just a memory. Those who had followed him to his last rest came straggling back into town. Coony Fyle went by with the hearse, heading for his livery barn. Buckboards, spring wagons, and riders drifted in and stopped here and there along the street. The surrey, with Clint Brandon driving, pulled up at the hotel, and all its occupants got out and went in. Billy Prior came along and unlocked his store.

Bois Renfro, with his wife and daughter on the seat with him, brought his buckboard down street and pulled up in front of the store. A raw-boned, beetle-browed man with a rumbling voice, he jerked his head at Carlin.

"Hello, Leach. Sad day. The kind I don't like."

He got down and went into the store. Carlin straightened to his feet, moved out beside the buckboard, tipped his hat.

"Mrs. Renfro — Dallas, how are you?"

Dallas Renfro had a wealth of auburn hair and wide gray eyes which shone with a quick vitality. She was understandably sober at this moment, however.

"I've been miserable," she told Carlin. "Been bawlng my eyes out. Bet I look terrible."

"No," differed Carlin, "you don't. You were born with a shine to you and you'll always be that way."

The gravity of her face broke a little and she measured him steadily with those direct, clear eyes. She sighed and shook her head.

"If I only knew when you were serious and when you were full of blarney. Also, I'm wondering about that split lip you're packing."

"We were talking about you, not me," he evaded.

She snfffed. "My friend, when you begin to dodge and duck like that, then I know you've been up to some sort of mischief. Been fighting, haven't you? And on a day like this. For shame!"

Carlin showed her a faint smile. "Ornery scoundrel, that's me."

Mrs. Renfro, a slender, quiet-faced woman, said, "You've been away, haven't you, Leach? Seems months since we saw you last."

"Four of them, Mrs. Renfro. Spent them up in the Warners, clearing up a little cattle chore for Billy Prior."

"It's good to see you back again. There was some talk about you having left the country entirely after, well — your trouble with Clint Brandon. I was sure those who said so were wrong."

"It's not easy to ride away from familiar trails and a few good friends," Carlin said. Then, his small smile showing again, he added, "Time treats this daughter of yours very generously."

Dallas colored hotly. "Whoever hit you hard enough to split your lip, also addled your wits, Mister Carlin."

Mrs. Renfro laughed softly. "Seems like old times, bearing you two ragging each other."

Bois Renfro came out, a small packet of mail in his hand. He paused for a moment beside Carlin. "Got a feeling that things are starting to stir under the leaves, Leach. What do you think?"

"Could be that time of year, Bois. We'll have to wait and see."

Renfro stood for a moment, looking straight ahead. Then he nodded. "If it wasn't for Martha Brandon, I wouldn't give a damn."

He climbed into the buckboard, lifted the reins and kicked off the brake. "You hear anything, Leach, drop out to the ranch and tell us about it."

Carlin watched the rig roll away, then turned and went into the store. Billy Prior had shed his coat and hat and was now squirming out of the unaccustomed confines of a stiff collar. He sighed with relief as he laid it aside.

"That's done with. A duty, but never a pleasant one. Didn't see you at the cemetery, Leach."

"No," said Carlin soberly. "I'm a rank coward where a woman's tears are con-

38

cerned. How did Mrs. Brandon take it, Billy?"

"Like the Spartan she is. Steel in that woman, Leach. To some, Dan might have shaped up as a rough, tough old blister, but he was Martha Brandon's man, and they'd seen a lot of life together. She'll shed tears, of course, but she'll never show them in public." Billy glanced at Carlin's bruised and swollen lip. "You've acquired something since I saw you last. Randall?"

Carlin nodded. "Over in the Skyhigh. He was just bound to start something."

The storekeeper's eyes showed a flash of reminiscent anger. "Contemptible whelp, that fellow."

There was a step at the door and Sam Desmond came in. Once a man of fairly imposing stature, he had now a flabbiness about him, of the spirit as well as the flesh — a softness due partly to advancing years, but mainly caused by a weakening and dulling of some vital spark.

To Leach Carlin it seemed that somewhere along the tough race of life, Sam Desmond had suddenly given up. It was as though some inner drive of ambition and purpose had abruptly burned itself out, leaving only the shell of a man who had turned weak and desperate for some stronger will to cling to.

Dan Brandon had supplied that will and strength and courage, and for years Sam Desmond had followed in Dan's shadow, bending and agreeing to every Brandon yes or no. In attitude, when away from Brandon, Desmond had tried to cover up this flabbiness of flesh and spirit with a pose of bluster that had fooled no one. Looking at the man now, Carlin wondered what Desmond would do with Dan Brandon no longer a strong oak to lean on.

Desmond seemed to read the thought behind Carlin's glance, for a faint flush touched his sagging cheeks and he made an effort to straighten and square his shoulders.

"Martha wants to see you, Carlin. Over at the hotel."

Startled, Carlin was still for a moment. "Why should she want to see me, Sam?"

Desmond hesitated slightly, then shrugged.

"I wouldn't know and she didn't say. She just asked me to locate you and tell you."

Carlin tipped his head. "Thanks, Sam. I'll go right over, of course."

He went out and cut along the street. Joe Spence and Jimmy Spurlock had drifted over to the Skyhigh again and were just turning in there, along with Hoot McLean and Buell Hadley. Angling for the hotel, Carlin's head was bent in thought. He couldn't imagine what was behind this summons.

In the foyer he came face to face with Clint Brandon and Beth Desmond. It did not in any way surprise him to see the open hate that moiled in Clint's dark eyes. For the last time he'd stood this close to Clint, it was to see Clint stretched flat on his back, beaten and bloody and unconscious, made so by the savage fury of Carlin's driving fists. That had been a black day all around, one never to be forgotten by either of them.

Clint made no pretense of speaking and Carlin looked past him at the girl.

"It's been some time, Beth — and good to see you again. Your father said Mrs. Brandon wanted to see me."

There had never been a time when the nearness of this girl had not had the power to stir him, and he'd been at a loss to fully analyze his feelings toward her. He admired her beauty; no man could help but do that. Yet, while she attracted him, she also filled him with a vague uneasiness, the cause of which he'd never been able to figure out.

She could be warmly charming and exciting, and she could also be cold and aloof. It was as if there were two of her, the one right before you, the other who stood far back, measuring all things with a cool, dispassionate calculation. She was a girl to intrigue and bewilder a man. Now she nodded and spoke.

"She's waiting for you in the parlor, Leach."

The parlor of the hotel was a small room, but comfortable in its furnishings. Martha Brandon was in here alone, seated in an armchair, and her voice came, low and a little weary.

"Close the door, Leach. And thank you for coming. I was afraid, all things considered, that I'd asked too much of you."

Carlin closed the door, then stood before her, silent and grave. He'd never been a glib man, and just now he could think of nothing to say. She looked up at him and understood.

"He's in green fields now, Leach. Come, pull up a chair beside me. And smoke, please."

Building a cigarette helped greatly in getting past the awkward moment. Carlin cleared his throat.

"I'm no hand at words, Mrs. Brandon. But I think you know how I feel."

She nodded her white head. "Yes, I know. You admired him greatly, didn't you — in spite of all that took place? Well, I want you to know it was a mutual feeling. Dan was wrong that day, greatly wrong. And admitted as much after you had gone." She looked at Carlin closely. "There's a fresh bruise on your mouth, Leach."

He shrugged. "Duff Randall. It's been brewing between us for a long time. It came into the open today."

She nodded again. "A number of things are going to come into the open. Some I can see clearly, others I can only guess at with reasonable certainty. All of which only goes to further cement my decision about the future of Hackamore."

She was silent for a thoughtful moment, then her request came with startling abruptness.

"Leach, I want you to come back to Hackamore and take over in complete charge."

Carlin went so still the thread of smoke seeping up from the tip of his cigarette cut a thin, straight, blue line. He had guessed at several reasons why Mrs. Brandon should have wanted to see him, but he'd not remotely considered anything like this. His words were stumbling when he finally managed an answer.

"Me — take over at Hackamore! Mrs. Brandon, you can't mean that. Clint would never stand for any part of it. Clint was the reason I had to leave Hackamore before and —"

"Yes, I know," she broke in. "Clint has been the reason for a lot of good men leaving Hackamore. But that was then and this is now. Clint doesn't own Hackamore. I do. And I have my own ideas of how I want the ranch run. The same way it was run by Dan Brandon in his younger years, when the challenge of life was a joyous thing to him, before he grew weary and sick at heart. And whether he likes it or not, Clint will have to go along with those ideas. Now, if you'll bear with me for a time, I'll explain a number of things which I think will make you understand Dan a little better and so forgive him for the unjust treatment he gave you toward the last."

Again she was silent for a little time, the expression in her eyes that of a person casting back over the memory of years that had been rich and great. Carlin's cigarette went out and he touched a freshening match to it.

"I'm going to tell you something, Leach," went on Martha Brandon presently, "something which no one on Big Sage Prairie except Dan and myself ever knew. It will surprise you and you will, of course, keep the knowledge strictly to yourself. Clint is not my natural son. He's an adopted one. Of the great sorrows of my life, one was my inability to bear children for Dan because he dearly wanted them, especially a son. To fill this void, we adopted Clint when he was only a few weeks old. His parents had lived in a mining camp, up in Idaho. His father had been killed in a mining accident, a cave-in, I believe it was, and his mother lived only a week or two after Clint was born. She was a distant relative of Dan's and before she died we got word of her condition through the kindness of a neighbor. Dan and I made a trip up there. We were afraid that the baby, so very young, might not be able to stand the trip back to Big Sage, so Dan came back without me and I stayed for several months, waiting for milder weather. When I returned, I brought Clint with me."

Once more she was silent, reviewing the years. She sighed softly.

"I believe I've the right to say I tried very hard to be a real mother to Clint. I gave him a mother's love and care. Dan idolized the boy, and many were the times I prayed that Clint would grow up into the kind of man Dan wanted him to be. But as the years went by I had to face the discouraging fact that what Dan hoped for in the boy simply wasn't there and never would be. I know that Dan, toward the end, realized this himself. Yet he'd built such great plans around Clint, and his initial pride in him had been so great — it was a hard thing to face, Leach."

She touched a hand to her eyes and Carlin waited in still gravity, wishing there was something he could do to soften the pain of this woman, while knowing that there wasn't. Martha Brandon straightened in her chair and again her snowy head lifted, fine and proud.

"So now we come to today, to Hackamore and its future. What is Hackamore, Leach? I see it as more than just another cattle ranch. I see it as a monument to a man, to my husband. This is a time to remember things and I'm remembering so much — so very much! I'm remembering the day Dan and I first set foot on Big Sage Prairie. We had a spring wagon, a team of horses, some gear and a little food. Our first home was a soddy dugout, not half as big as this room. But we had each other and we had our dreams. We went through hardships unbelievable. It was like climbing some tremendous mountain, foot by precious foot, with every step a battle. But we climbed that mountain, Leach. Dan and I climbed it. We built Hackamore!"

Now she got to her feet and paced up and

down the room. Despite the hardship and toil her life had known, there was still a certain grace in her movements, and the remnants of a beauty which, though faded with the years, still glowed like some inextinguishable fire.

"Yes, Leach — we built Hackamore. We toiled and suffered and fought, and it was never easy. So now, Hackamore stands as a strong monument to Dan Brandon. And I'm not going to allow it to be torn down."

She came to a stop, facing Carlin.

"Left in Clint's hands and management, it would be torn down. For Clint hasn't the fiber and courage to hold it together. He hasn't the character. He's selfish and self-centered. He is also — and God knows I hate to have to admit this — sly and untrustworthy. Does it make me less of a mother to say such things? No matter — they must be said, for they are true, and today is a day for truth.

"I know what some men are thinking, Leach — men like Case Broderick and Mike Quarney. They think, now that Dan is gone, Hackamore is a golden sheep, ready for the shearing. They think that Clint will take over, and so make it easy for them. They'd be correct in this, if Clint was allowed to take over. He'd never stand up to them. I

47

doubt if he'd really try, because he has no particular affection for Hackamore as such, nor for what it stands for. It would be like him to argue for a little time, and then arrange some sort of deal by which he'd get enough for himself without too much struggle or effort, and with never a second thought or regret for what Hackamore means to me and to the memory of the man who tried so hard to be a good father to him.

"Oh, I know Clint — I know him so very well. And he is not going to have Hackamore to waste and destroy. More than once in the past I've heard men say that Dan Brandon rode a tough saddle. Now I want another man strong enough to take over that tough saddle. And, Leach, I'm asking you to be the man!"

Now it was Carlin's turn to get to his feet and pace the room. Martha Brandon watched him, waiting for him to turn the thing over in his mind, to weigh all the angles, to visualize what lay ahead, should he accept. His eyes were shadowed, his face graven. She added further persuasion.

"There are limits to what a woman can do, Leach. She can hold true to a trust and, in her own way, fight for it tenaciously. But in a case of this sort things can move to a point where a woman is helpless. Only a man can take over at that stage of a battle. And if you are wondering why I'm asking you to be that man, Leach, I'll give you at least a few of the reasons.

"Over the years, several men acted as foreman of Hackamore. None handled the job as you did, not half as well, nor with the personal interest you showed. I'm remembering a day when Dan said to me that you were the one man he was confident he could leave in control of Hackamore for any period of time and come back to find the ranch thriving and sound. The fact that you and he came to disagreement in the end does not change that opinion. For the trouble was not your fault, nor wholly Dan's either. The fault was Clint's. And believe me, Leach — I'm not asking all this of you out of personal selfishness. There will be a reward for you, perhaps far greater than you dream."

Carlin stopped his pacing, drew a deep breath and looked at her levelly. "I wasn't even considering that angle, Mrs. Brandon. About any particular personal reward, I mean. But I was looking at some of the things certain to lie ahead. One of these is that Clint will buck me at every turn of the trail."

"Yes," she agreed quietly, "he will. At least he'll try to. But I'll back you, Leach.

You'll have my complete and unswerving support, no matter what comes. I wouldn't ask you to take over such a responsibility and then tie your hands with any wavering allegiance."

"There would," he reminded her, "be times when I'd have to get rough. Maybe even with Clint. And no one can say right now how far that roughness might reach, or what it could lead to."

She knew exactly what he meant. "I saw Dan get rough, savagely so, many times, Leach. But when a man is right and roughness is the only solution, then roughness is justified. I'll not fail you there, either."

Carlin now spoke softly, as though putting his thoughts aloud. "Hackamore was my ideal of a ranch — all that a ranch should be. I had a lot of pride in working for it before. When I had to leave, it knocked a lot of purpose in life out of me. It would be good to be back — good!"

Martha Brandon dropped a hand on his arm. "I knew you felt that way about us, Leach. The nearest Dan and I ever came to a real quarrel was that day you thrashed Clint and Dan discharged you. For it was Clint's fault — all of it. I knew it and Dan knew it. Yet Clint had a way of moving Dan against his better judgment. But he never could and never will be able to do the same with me. Leach, come back to Hackamore."

He looked at her and she held his eyes bravely. And what he saw in hers was a trust and judgment that would never let him down. He covered her hand with his own and spoke a little huskily.

"All right, Mrs. Brandon — I'll come back."

She caught at him, dropped her white head against him. Her voice was muffled. "Thank you, Leach — thank you. And now, if you don't mind, I think I need this shoulder of yours for a little time."

She wept then. It was the bursting grief that had piled up inside of her and it had to come out. It was better so, and Carlin, realizing this, put an arm about her shoulders and waited quietly for the storm to pass. Gradually it did so, and then she moved away from him, dabbing with a handkerchief at her eyes and nose. Presently she turned and her head was up once more and she smiled at him bravely.

"I think we understand each other, Leach — you and I. You'll come out to Hackamore right away?"

"I'll be out this evening."

Someone knocked at the door, sharply insistent. Carlin stepped over and opened it.

Case Broderick stood there. He stared at Carlin in surprise and with frank hostility, then spoke curtly.

"I've something to discuss with Mrs. Brandon."

Before Carlin could answer, Martha Brandon spoke. "Very well, Mr. Broderick. You may say what you have to say in front of Leach. He is my good and trusted friend. What is it you wish?"

Case Broderick was plainly disconcerted at Carlin's presence. His hesitancy became a lengthening, taut silence. His glance swung from Carlin to Martha Brandon, then back to Carlin, who met it bleakly.

"You got something to say, Broderick — get it done!"

Broderick shrugged, stepped past Carlin to the center of the small room. He spread his feet, squared himself, almost as though preparing to throw some kind of physical blow. His voice took on an edge of roughness.

"What I have to say won't take long. It has to do with that piece of range lying between Steptoe Creek and the Indian Mounds. Brandon hogged that range from other men, me included. Now I intend to take it back. I don't want to start any trouble over it, but if I have to, I will. You have a week in which to move all Hackamore cattle off that range. Then I move in and occupy."

"You and other men, you say," murmured Carlin. "Would one of them be Mike Quarney?"

Broderick neither answered this nor turned around. But the back of his neck showed a tide of betraying red.

Martha Brandon was looking Broderick up and down with a cool and distant scorn which made him begin to shift restlessly. When she spoke, her words were as cutting as her glance.

"You grow brave don't you, Mister Broderick, now that my husband is no longer here to defend Hackamore interests? And you lack the simple decency of allowing me even a few short days for readjustment. Well, I've a surprise in store for you, Mister Broderick. As of this moment Leach Carlin is foreman and manager of Hackamore, with full and unquestioned authority to act as he thinks best. He has my complete confidence and backing. I turn you over to him for your answer."

If Case Broderick had been disconcerted before, he was now doubly so. He swung around to face Carlin and for once his cold eyes reflected a jarred uncertainty.

"So that's it!" he blurted.

Carlin's smile was faint, mirthless. "Yeah — that's it!" He'd never liked Broderick. Now he despised the man, for Broderick had clearly shown that he'd entered this room with the intent to threaten and bully the widow, callous of her loss and grief. He knew a sharp exultancy at this chance to tell the fellow off.

"The range you speak of, Broderick, has always been Hackamore grass. When you or anybody else say otherwise, you lie! Any range Dan Brandon ever took over, he took fairly. And what now belongs to Hackamore stays that way. You just mentioned the word "trouble." Well, start some and you'll choke on what you stir up. There's your answer. Now — get out!"

Broderick's first stunned surprise was passing and anger took its place. It came out of his eyes, bleak and bitter.

"We'll see. Clint will have something to say about this. And he'll stand to see the fair thing done."

"To the contrary," retorted Martha Brandon. "Clint will have nothing to say about it. At least, nothing that will in any way change the facts Leach has just given you."

"I guess that's all of it, Broderick," said Carlin. "You wanted an answer and you got one. That way is out!" He stabbed a pointing finger at the door.

Case Broderick stood his ground for a moment, then turned to go. At the door he paused to say something he'd said before.

"We'll see."

Carlin grinned mockingly and closed the door in his face.

When Carlin left the hotel and stepped into Bidwell Street again, the afternoon had run its full warm length. The sun had dropped beyond the Warners, leaving behind a broad band of autumn sunset color. Twilight filled Modoc City with a smoky, blue stillness and a welcome breath of coolness came in with the deepening shadow. Carlin walked slowly to the Skyhigh, where Ace Lanier had already lighted up his hanging lamps.

There was a fair crowd in the saloon. Buell Hadley, Hoot McLean, and Sam Desmond were there, having a quiet drink together. Further along a little group of Hackamore riders were doing the same thing. Over at a card table Joe Spence and Jimmy Spurlock were playing cribbage. As Carlin entered and moved down the room, Buell Hadley crooked a finger.

"Have one on me, Leach."

Carlin dropped in beside him and said to Ace Lanier, "Just a short one."

Hadley said, "Understand you've been taking care of a job for Billy Prior, Leach. If that's done with and you're looking for something else, drop out my way. I can use you."

Carlin was silent while Ace Lanier poured and shoved the glass across. Then he shook his head.

"Thanks, Buell. But Mrs. Brandon has put in first call."

This brought immediate attention through the room.

"Yeah?" exclaimed Hadley. "How's that?"

"She asked me to come back to Hackamore and take over in complete charge. I agreed to do it."

Sam Desmond, who was listening intently, upset his whiskey glass and then swore with unnecessary vehemence to cover up the incident. Hoot McLean, a gaunt, lantern-jawed, sorrel-topped Scotsman, barked a short, gusty laugh, and when Carlin looked at him questioningly, explained.

"I was just thinking what a jolt that will be to some I could name, Leach."

Buell Hadley took the news quietly. "Now that I think on it, it doesn't surprise me too much. Martha Brandon is a long-headed woman. You ramrodded the ranch before,

Leach, so you know the layout thoroughly. I'm saying that she made a damn smart choice."

"Where's that going to leave Clint?" asked Sam Desmond. "What's he going to think about it?"

Desmond was staring straight ahead, a blot of hectic color in either cheek. Carlin glanced at him, then shrugged. "I wouldn't know, Sam." He rang a coin on the bar. "Another round, Ace."

The little group of Hackamore hands had abruptly ceased their idle talk. Now they broke up and left the place, their spurs scuffing.

"Among others," said Hoot McLean, "I can think of who'll hardly celebrate this news, Leach, I'd say that Mike Quarney and Case Broderick may lose some sleep over it." Hoot lifted his glass. "To Mrs. Brandon — a very wise woman!"

Sam Desmond drank with them, but his hand was shaking so he spilled half the liquor in his glass. Hoot McLean looked at him in mild wonder. "Man," he growled, "can't you master the stuff? Leach, it's my turn to buy."

Carlin put down his glass and shook his head. "Some other time, Hoot. Right now I got things to do."

He moved over to the card table and

looked down at Joe Spence and Jimmy Spurlock with a faint, dry grin.

"You used to ride for Hackamore, you two. Then you both got fired, proving the pair of you are more or less worthless. But I'd kind of like to have you around again out at Hackamore. Interested?"

Joe Spence swept the cards together. "Now, there's an idea. At least I'd be sure of eating regular again."

Jimmy Spurlock looked up at Carlin soberly. "It would be like going home again, Leach," he admitted. "But I'm warning you. I just can't get along with Clint."

"You won't have to, kid. But you will have to get along with me."

"That," declared Jimmy, "I can do. When do you want me and Joe to show up?"

"Tomorrow morning will be all right. By that time there should be a couple of empty bunks ready for you."

Joe Spence cocked an inquiring eye. "Could it be that some now riding for Hackamore are due to leave?"

Carlin grinned more widely, reached out and jerked Joe's hat down over his eyes.

"You should roost in the trees with the rest of the wise old owls, Joe. See you at Hackamore!"

CHAPTER THREE

Coming up to Hackamore through the wide, shadowed peace of early night, Leach Carlin was traveling a well-remembered trail, one that he had covered many, many times during the three years he'd ramrodded the ranch. They'd been three good years, probably the fullest and most satisfying of his life. For Hackamore was the kind of layout a man could get his teeth into. Working it, a man knew he had hold of something really worthwhile; something with foundations that were sound and secure, on which to build almost without limit.

Carlin had known a deep, quiet pride in his job, in being able to produce to Dan Brandon's satisfaction. But then there had come a covert and growing animosity on the part of Clint Brandon. Envious apparently, of Carlin's authority and prestige as Hackamore's foreman, Clint had set to work in his smooth, dark way to undermine Carlin in the eyes of Dan Brandon and, as Martha Brandon had said, Clint had a way of moving old Dan against his own better judgment.

In no way fooled at any time, Carlin knew what Clint was up to and, for as long as he could, ignored Clint's devious scheming. Cllnt, growing bolder, edged more into the open. He countermanded Carlin's orders. He rawhided certain of Carlin's better riders, driving them to quit or to some act of insubordination that caused old Dan to fire them. He hired others who would follow him and not Carlin.

In the light of such conditions, it was inevitable that the smooth running of ranch affairs should suffer, and Dan Brandon finally took Carlin to task for it. Had he felt that matters would have been permanently bettered by his taking the blame, Carlin would have done so and let it go at that. But he knew that Clint was not to be stopped that way. So he stood his ground and flatly stated Clint's part in the trouble. Clint, denying much of it, called Carlin out of name and in a burst of black anger Carlin had thrashed Clint savagely. That made the end inevitable.

As he had told Martha Brandon, leaving Hackamore had knocked a lot of purpose out of life for Leach Carlin. For despite the domineering crustiness that was so much a part of Dan Brandon, Carlin had seen past this front to the real man underneath, and had found there much to respect and admire. So it hurt deeply to have the old man turn against him, particularly in unjust judgment. Also, he was the sort to put a great deal of himself into any project he tackled, and he had done this at Hackamore. Thus, when he left, there was much he had given that he could not take away with him.

Hearing that Clint was not the natural son of Dan and Martha Brandon had been a surprise. Yet, on thinking it over, this fact explained many things to Carlin. For he had never been able to reconcile Clint's slipperiness with the rugged honesty of his parents. Now he knew that Clint hadn't come from such worth-while stock. Clint had different blood in him and it wasn't good blood.

There had been another angle, too. There had been Beth Desmond. Once Leach Carlin had thought that he'd seen in her image something of the ideal every man carried in his secret heart. Perhaps even a shadow of that thought still lingered, but here, too, the advantage had gone to Clint. Beth and Clint put in more and more time together, an arrangement which seemed to suit Sam Desmond, at least, extremely well. So it was that when Carlin left Hackamore, it was a dismal realization of complete loss that he'd carried away with him.

Now he was coming back! Things would not be the same, of course. The powerful shadow of Dan Brandon no longer lay across the ranch. It would be a big chore to measure up to the responsibilities that would wait at every turn. Clint would still be Clint, certain to be more antagonistic than ever. But Martha Brandon had vowed her unswerving support, and she was not the sort to falter or take back her word.

Carlin watched the lights of the ranch grow in the night ahead and from old practice could identify each one of them — those in the office and various rooms of the ranch house, and those in the bunkhouse and cook shack. Then there was the dark loom of the barns and feed sheds and other lesser ranch buildings. There were the shadowy outlines of the corral fences in the thin light of the early stars. And there was the black line of growth along Tempest Creek, where it broke from the Warners and thrust for the open country beyond.

All of these things were as familiar to Carlin as the palm of his hand, and he pulled his horse to a stop by a corner of a lower corral while he savored this old and well-remembered scene. Then he rode on along and stopped in front of the saddle shed. He swung down, untied his frugal warbag of possessions from behind the saddle cantle, hooked a stirrup over the horn and began loosening the latigo. Then it was that Clint Brandon's voice came at him from the dark.

"Better think it over good, Carlin — before you go any further!"

Carlin went still for a moment, then came around to face Clint, who stepped out past the corner of the shed.

"I've done my thinking, Clint. I'm here."

"Yeah, you're here, where you got no right to be. And where I don't want you."

"I'm here at your mother's express wish," retorted Carlin quietly. "I'm staying until she says different."

Clint's voice had been reasonably even. Now it took on a hard and angry note. "I've got rights around here and I've got authority. Now I'm telling you to load that gear back on your saddle and get out. Get off Hackamore land — and stay off!"

"I'm not listening, Clint."

"You damn well better listen!" The angry note in Clint's voice turned thin and raging. "No damned two-bit hard case is moving in and euchering me out of anything. Take your junk and get out!"

Clint had moved in closer. Now he kicked over Carlin's warbag. He pulled off his hat and swung it at the head of Carlin's horse.

The startled animal reared back, pulled away from Carlin, who let it go.

The dregs of an older anger burst into a glow in Carlin. Harshly he said, "You damned fool!" Then he look a long stride forward, locked a hand in the front of Clint's shirt and put the drive of his shoulder behind a stiffened arm. He slammed Clint up against the front of the saddle shed and held him there.

Clint was solidly built and was far from a physical weakling. He tried to struggle free and when he couldn't make it, swung a couple of pawing blows at Carlin's head. But Carlin was of rangier build and the length of Carlin's stiffened arm was such that by pulling his head back slightly, he avoided Clint's fists. With his left hand, Carlin cuffed down Clint's pawing fists, jerked him forward, then slammed him back against the shed again — hard!

"You damned fool!" rapped Carlin again. "Do I have to make the new start here by cutting you down to size once more? Well, I'll do it if you don't listen to sense. So right here and now you and me come down to cases. I know it's useless to hope that you'd work along with me for the good of Hackamore. You're just not a big enough man to put aside your personal feelings and do that. You cut the ground from under me once before. Well, you won't do it this time and I think you know it. Just the same, we're going to make sure. In a few minutes you and me are going in to face your mother. We'll both listen to what she has to say. We're going to have it plain, direct from her, just where you stand and where I stand. But first let's get this other fact straight, finally and for good."

He jerked Clint away from the shed wall, then slammed him back into it again. Clint cursed with a thick and helpless fury. Carlin was inexorable.

"I thrashed hell out of you once before. But what you got then was just a thin shadow of what you'll get if you try and double-deal me again. I didn't take on this job with the idea that I was signing for a soft ride. I know it's going to be a rough one, so I'm not going to spare the quirt or the spurs. I'll stamp roughshod over any man who tries to block my trail. That in cludes you. So you better come to your feed, Clint, and recognize some of the hard facts of life!"

He could feel the rage that was shaking Clint and he realized bleakly that there wasn't now, and never would be, any slightest chance of bringing Clint to time. They were at opposite poles and there could never be any agreement between them. He pushed Clint aside and stepped back.

"As soon as I've finished unsaddling, I'm going over to the office. You be there, Clint. Then we'll hear what your mother has to say."

He turned and went after his horse, which had stopped beside the corral gate. He stripped off saddle and headstall, turned the animal into the corral. When he came back to the shed with his saddle, Clint was gone. Over at the ranch house a door slammed.

Carlin stood for a time, building a cigarette. Now, all about him the headquarters was silent. Almost too quiet, even though it was a place where death had lately struck. There was a sense of waiting here. Over in the bunkhouse, Carlin knew, were men Clint had hired on, after driving older hands to quit. They would be Clint's men, ready to do his bidding above all others.

Carlin took a couple of deep drags at his cigarette, then went over to the ranch house. The office was a corner room with one window facing the town trail and another which looked out at the corrals and various secondary buildings. By this window there was an outside door. Light shone in the room and as Carlin moved up to the door he looked in and saw Martha Brandon sitting quietly at the desk that had been her husband's. Carlin knocked and her summons called him in. Her smile was grave and steady.

"I was sure it was you, Leach. I'd thought to go through some of Dan's papers, but I find a lot here that have to do with ranch affairs I'm not familiar with. I'm going to turn it all over to you to work out. You saw Clint — outside?"

Carlin nodded, a question in his glance.

"I guessed he'd be waiting for you," she sighed. "We had quite a scene earlier this evening when I told him of my plans for you. It wasn't — pleasant. He's going to be difficult, Leach."

Carlin took off his hat and tossed it in a corner. "I can handle him, Mrs. Brandon — if you want it that way."

She studied him gravely. In the lamp glow the ruggedness of his features made a study in shadow and highlight. His hair was thick and brown, with a certain unruliness about it that made for strength. She held his glance very steadily.

"I want it that way, Leach. I told you how I felt. I haven't changed. I'll never change."

"I'm sure of that," said Carlin. "Yet it would help, I think, if you'd call Clint in here and put it plainly just where he stands and just where I stand. Then he can never claim any misunderstanding."

"Very well." She got up and went to an inner door which opened into the ranch house proper, and sent a clear-voiced call along a hall. "Clint! Please come into the office."

She turned back to Carlin and pointed at a chair behind the desk. "Sit there, Leach. That chair belongs to the master of this ranch."

As Carlin sat down, she moved over to a window and stared out at the unrevealing night. Presently she turned. "Just as if it were your ranch, Leach — that's the way I want you to take hold."

Steps sounded along the hall and Clint came in. He'd got control of himself again. His face was still and dark and smooth as ever, but the residue of his anger lay in a slight flush across his cheeks and burned far back in his black eyes. Martha Brandon spoke almost gently.

"There is nothing I'd like better than an amicable understanding with you, Clint. But something must be understood. The man who sits behind that desk runs Hackamore. His word is law and authority on this ranch. I know it will be for the general good of Hackamore. I hope to bring you to acknowledge that fact."

Clint's stare touched Carlin, then moved to his mother. "That's what you brought me in here for?"

"Yes, Clint."

He turned away. "It don't mean a thing to me." The door clicked shut behind him.

Martha Brandon looked at Carlin and a thread of bitterness came into her voice. "At least he told the truth there, and that's the whole trouble. The ranch, as such, doesn't mean a thing to him. He doesn't see it as something to hold on to, to build on and to make more secure. He sees it as just something he'd like to convert into money, ready money. I'm afraid it just isn't in Clint to be true to anything or anyone, not even himself. Is that a terrible thing to say, Leach, even by a foster mother?"

"Not when it is the truth and needs to be said, Mrs. Brandon. And it takes a real brand of courage to say it."

"Thank you, Leach. Now, I would ask one last favor of you. In things that count, don't give an inch with Clint. But in those which do not count too greatly, be as patient with him as you can. For the sake of Dan's memory, if nothing else."

He met her glance and saw in it the shadow of a great loneliness. He also saw the glimmer

69

of tears and his voice ran very quiet. "I understand, Mrs. Brandon. I'll give Clint every break I can."

She turned away to stare out of the window again and Carlin, to cover up the moment, rummaged busily in the desk, coming up with Dan Brandon's time and check books.

"Could be that some of the present crew will be leaving," he said. "If you'll sign two or three checks, I'll fill in the amount of wages due."

She faced him again. "You may sign them, Leach. I arranged that matter with Lyle Barnard before leaving town. From now on the bank will honor any Hackamore check signed by you."

For a moment Carlin did not know what to say. Then his voice ran low and gruff. "That's a lot of trust, Mrs. Brandon."

She smiled. "There is no such thing as trusting halfway, Leach. Either you trust a person completely, or you don't trust him at all."

He got his hat and moved to the outer door. She came over beside him and dropped a hand on his arm. "Had Dan lived, he'd have gone on building, Leach."

Carlin nodded. "We'll go on building, Mrs. Brandon."

He went over to the saddle shed and gathered up his warbag. Then he strode over to the bunkhouse and went in. A stir ran through the several riders who were there. Plainly they had been expecting him, some enigmatic and still of face, others with an unsure restlessness. Carlin chose an empty bunk, piled his gear on it. Then he straightened and let his glance run over the room.

"Changes have taken place," he said curtly. "Mrs. Brandon has hired me to run Hackamore. From now on you'll take your orders from me — all of them."

A rider on a bunk near the door, spoke with a studied insolence. "Clint's been giving me my orders. That still suits me."

Carlin nodded, as though he'd heard what he expected to hear. "You can roll your gear, Labine. You're leaving us."

There was a round-topped table, littered with cards and other odds and ends. Carlin pulled a chair up to it, swept an open place with the palm of his hand, put time and check books there and began to figure. He could feel the stare of every man in the room, but outwardly appeared completely oblivious to them. Boot heels scraped angrily on the floor and the voice of Frank Labine hit at him.

"Only one man can order me off this

71

ranch, and that's Clint Brandon. So far he hasn't."

Carlin did not even look up. "Roll your gear. You're leaving. I think Ward Dancy might as well roll his, too. He wouldn't feel right without you to tail along after."

These two, Frank Labine and Ward Dancy, had been Clint's men and had helped Clint undermine him, back at the time of the original blow-up. It was plain from Labine's words and attitude that there'd be no change for the better here. There was only one thing to do, and that was to get rid of them.

Carlin completed his figuring. It wasn't difficult. Dan Brandon had always been meticulous with his paper work. The records were complete, the facts all there. Carlin wrote out two checks, fanned them in the air to dry them, then got to his feet.

Ward Dancy had the nearest bunk. He was a thin, slack, medium-sized man, with a sharp, narrow face and a lock of black hair which lay slantwise across his forehead. He was making no move, plainly awaiting the outcome of Frank Labine's defiance. Carlin dropped a check on the bunk beside Dancy, then moved on and did the same with Labine.

"You can make it easy or rough on yourself, Frank," he said.

Labine, burly, pock-marked, with a stiff roach of coarse, early-grizzled hair, brushed the check off the bunk to the floor. "Hell with you!"

Carlin's eyes pinched down, a gust of anger roughening his cheeks. "Rough it is!"

He reached down, hauled Labine erect. Labine hit his feet fighting. He brought up an inside fist that slammed into Carlin's jaw, jarring him back on his heels, and Labine followed this advantage with a whining eagerness. From the door of the bunkhouse came Clint Brandon's voice.

"That's it, Frank — that's it! Work the proud bastard over!"

Frank Labine was willing. He clubbed a left to the side of Carlin's head, then put everything he had into a sweeping right. Carlin stepped inside the swing and hit Labine under the heart, a lifting, powerful blow. Labine gasped and sagged back, his guard dropping. Instantly Carlin's fists were up, chopping at Labine's face. A whipping left to the mouth brought leaping crimson, and then a smashing right under the eye spun Labine half off his feet.

Labine reeled, caught his balance, wrapped his head in his arm and lunged forward, trying to get in close. Carlin caught him by the shoulders and swung him past. This, with the impetus of Labine's rush, sent the rider crashing into the bunkhouse wall. And when he bounced off and turned, badly jarred and shaken up, Carlin was waiting there to cut him down with three blazing, wicked punches. Labine sagged to one knee, his hands spread on the floor to keep from going all the way down.

Further along the bunkouse the watching Ward Dancy sighed, hauled his warbag from under his bunk and began packing it.

Still on one knee, Labine tipped up a bloody face and peered at Carlin out of his right eye. The left one was already swelling shut.

"You're a tough bucko, Carlin," he mumbled thickly, "but there's always another time."

On the second try he lurched to his feet and over to his bunk. Here he rested a moment, then began getting his gear together. Carlin picked the check off the floor and dropped it on Labine's bunk again.

"Don't want you to forget this, Frank. Just so you won't feel that Hackamore owes you anything. Remember, you could have made it easier for yourself."

There was a taut period of silence while

Labine and Dancy finished packing their gear. When they went out, Labine leading the way, Clint still stood in the doorway. He said something in a low, curtly angry voice. Labine shouldered past him without answering and Ward Dancy was equally silent. Leach Carlin looked around at the remaining crew members.

"If any of the rest of you don't like the new picture, now's the time to step out and say so."

They were silent a moment. Then one of them stirred. "Far as I'm concerned, Labine was just talking for himself."

Carlin watched the others nod concurrence to this. "Fair enough," he said. "We're starting with a clean slate. All you have to do is put your full allegiance behind Hackamore, do your work, and you'll get a square shake from me."

He turned and looked at Clint, who had moved out on the bunkhouse step where, half in light, half in dark, he stood staring toward the corrals after Frank Labine and Ward Dancy. Feeling Carlin's glance, Clint squared around and returned it with a stark, flat hatred.

"The air needed clearing, Clint," said Carlin mildly.

Clint turned and plunged off into the

night. A little later, hoofs rocketed away from the ranch.

In the largest and most pretentious dwelling in Modoc City, a house standing well back from the southern end of Bidwell Street, ex-Senator Mike Quarney was entertaining company in a room he chose to call his law study. Shelves of law books and bulky volumes of the Congressional Record lined the walls. In the center of the room, under a cone of light from a hanging lamp, a big, flat-topped desk held space. On the four walls of the room, where the book shelves offered clearance, hung pictures of Washington, Jefferson, and Lincoln, and a framed copy of the Declaration of Independence.

Mike Quarney himself was a spare, tall man with a flowing mane of hair that had now begun to thin badly. In his younger years and at the peak of his political life, he'd been known as "Handsome" Mike Quarney which sobriquet he'd borne with great pride and a distinct flair. But time and the pace of hard living had had their inevitable way with Mike Quarney. Years of overfondness for rye whiskey had veined his cheeks, and the sagging folds of skin under his chin formed a dewlap. The famed eagle look of his youth had degenerated into a sharpness of feature that was predatory and gaunt. The lips that rolled the inevitable cigar were thin and down-curving and the eyes that bracketed the beaked nose were hard and crafty and calculating.

Seated behind the desk in a worn, leather-lined chair, he looked across at his visitor, Case Broderick. On the desk was a bottle of rye whiskey, two glasses, and a half-emptied box of cigars. Also a long, legal-sized envelope. Quarney leaned forward and tapped this with a bony forefinger.

"There it is," he said. "The word we've been waiting for. The authority will be passed. It will be a rider on the main appropriation bill. Which is a break for us, as it will attract much less publicity that way than if it had come out under a separate appropriation, named for a specific job. This way it will take longer for the word to get around and so give us an edge in time. Which we can't afford to waste. For, should the opposition hear of the matter, they could be twice as hard to handle. What have you got to suggest?"

Broderick spread his hands. "Nothing different from what we first planned, Mike. Move in and take over. But it won't be easy, now. It might have been fairly so, once. I thought the biggest break of luck in the world had come our way when Brandon died. Then Martha Brandon had to spring this joker on us."

"You mean hiring on Leach Carlin?"

Broderick nodded. "That's it."

Quarney scratched a match, sucked moistly on his cigar. "Only one man."

"True enough," agreed Broderick. "But he can be a rough one. We'd be fools not to recognize and admit that. It would have been simple enough to handle Clint. A strong bluff, then an offer to buy at a nominal price, and Clint would have grabbed at the chance to get out without any farther trouble. But it's a different picture now, Mike. You can't put Leach Carlin in the same kennel with Clint."

Quarney leaned back, slouching a little in his chair. His eyes, small and cold, peered through the lifting smoke of his cigar.

"Big stakes," he said, "never come easy. And any man aiming at big stakes is a fool to turn squeamish. If what you say of Carlin is true, and I agree that it probably is, then one of our frst and most important moves is to get rid of the man."

"How?"

Into Mike Quarney's eyes came a flicker of pure malevolence. "How do you get rid of anything you don't want around? You wipe it out — you kill it!"

Case Broderick stirred restlessly, was silent while he built and lit a cigarette. Quarney straightened in his chair and leaned across the table.

"Did I say something about turning squeamish? Well, we'll have none of that, Case. I've done a lot of planning toward this thing. I've put in time and thought and money. Tim's my brother but it's cost me plenty of money to keep him at the capital, promoting matters, pushing this thing, keeping me advised. Now it is going through and I intend to cash in on it. And the insignificance of one man's life isn't going to stand between me and what I've planned for so long. First, the big project. After that, I wipe the name of Hackamore off the face of Big Sage Prairie. I'm a good hater, Case. You just said it was a lucky break for us when Brandon died. Maybe. But I think I would have liked him to have lived, so I could have watched him squirm and suffer while I broke him. Yeah, I'd have liked that."

Broderick shrugged. "Hell, Mike — I'm not backing away. I'm just adding up the facts we have to face."

Quarney settled back in his chair again, his manner going affable. "That's fine, Case — that's fine! Just remember this. We're in this

79

together, and we win or lose together. Now, another thought comes to me. I always believe in using any tools that are handy. I'm thinking of Clint Brandon."

Broderick spoke with open contempt. "Nothing to lean on there, Mike. No metal there at all."

Quarney gave out with a mirthless laugh. "The very reason he could be of value to us. This new setup at Hackamore is bound to be gall and wormwood to him. He's always hated Carlin — now he'll be red-eyed. And when you find a fellow like Clint feeling that way, he's open to any number of suggestions. Also, how's Duff Randall feeling? I hear that Carlin really worked him over."

"Duff bought himself something there. He's always fancied himself at rough and tumble. Now, after the way Carlin handled him, he's packing a long hate."

"Fine — fine," exulted Quarney comfortably, "exactly what we want. We'll be able to use that hate. No telling what it might lead to. Even to getting rid of Carlin. Sure, Randall rides for you. But if he should do for Carlin and any uncomfortable questions be asked, you can always point to the mauling Carlin handed him and pass it all off as just a matter of personal vengeance. That's what fools like Randall are for, Case — to be used by smarter men."

Case Broderick had always believed himself to be about as ruthless as they came, and knew a somewhat twisted pride in the fact. But just now, looking at this man across the desk from him, he realized what real ruthlessness was. Mike Quarney would use any man to his own advantage, and then leave that man to dangle, without qualm or concern. A faint chill went up Broderick's spine, and he stirred restlessly again. He pointed to the envelope on the desk.

"That word stays strictly between the two of us, Mike?"

"Exactly! Just the two of us."

"And we agree on our first move?"

"That's right," nodded Quarney, "what you laid in front of Martha Brandon. The Steptoe Creek–Indian Mounds range. Should we back away from that demand after making it, we'd be half licked to start with. That we have to have. We'll throw cattle on that land. A hundred–two hundred head. That should force Hackamore's hand, put the pressure on them."

Quarney's badly mauled cigar had gone out again. He took it from his lips, surveyed it a moment, then threw it aside. He took a fresh one from the box, lit up.

"We must realize, Case, that possession of that stretch of range at the right time is going to be the big nine points of law men speak of. We'll be realistic. We'll assume that Hackamore is going to put up a real fight on this deal. If that should happen, the noise of it might reach as far as Washington. And in that event we got brother Tim right there, right on the ground, ready to represent our side. Tim's made a lot of contacts, knows his way around in politics. What can Hackamore offer against that? Nothing! So, get the cattle on that ground. We hold the big cards."

Quarney reached for bottle and glasses, poured the drinks. He lifted his glass. "Looking at success, Case," he said.

From Quarney's house, Case Broderick walked along Bidwell Street toward the center of town, where he'd left his horse. The stars were big and bright in a sky that had turned cold, what with the night wind that had begun to sweep down from the Warners. Broderick was nearing the Skyhigh when two riders pulled in at the hitch rail there. As they dismounted, he heard one of them speak thickly.

"I need a drink. I need two or three drinks. That damned Carlin — !"

Watching them push through the saloon

door, Broderick recognized Frank Labine and Ward Dancy. Labine moved stiffly and in the brief glance Broderick got of Labine's face in the outpour of lamplight as the door winnowed, he saw that it was dark with bruises.

Broderick stood for a few moments, considering. He was remembering what Mike Quarney had just said about fools being made for the use of smarter men. A thin, hard smile touched his lips and he turned into the Skyhigh. He dropped in beside Labine and Dancy at the bar, nodding casually.

"Evening, boys. Thinking of a last one to keep me company on the ride home. Join me?"

They eyed him without speaking, Labine with only one good eye, the left being black-and-blue, and swollen shut. It was Labine who grunted and nodded acceptance to Broderick's offer to treat. After gulping the drink, Labine pulled a check from his pocket and spread it on the bar.

"How about cashing this, Lanier?" he growled.

Ward Dancy laid a similar check beside Labine's. "Make it two, Ace."

Ace Lanier glanced at the checks, took a closer look. "How come?" he demanded.

"Hackamore checks signed by Leach Carlin. They good?"

"Must be," said Dancy. "Frank and me got paid off with them."

Ace Lanier considered a moment, shrugged, and went down to the far end of the bar, where a small, iron safe stood. Case Broderick spoke softly.

"Paid off, eh? Any immediate future plans, boys?"

Ward Dancy shrugged. "Up to Frank."

"Jobs open for you at Circle 60, if you're interested," said Broderick. "And," he added, "a chance to get back at Carlin."

Frank Labine stared at the back bar mirror with his sound eye. "How?"

"He's the big man out at Hackamore now, so I understand. Things could be stirring to cut him down to size. Thought you might be interested in having a hand in that."

Labine considered for a moment, then his lips pulled into a harsh and ugly line. "A deal, Broderick. See you out there tomorrow."

"That," said Broderick, "calls for another drink — on me."

Back in the house at the south end of Bidwell Street, Mike Quarney sat for some time after Case Broderick left, pulling on his cigar and musing over his plans. He took the enclosure from the envelope and read it over again, satisfaction glinting in his eyes. Finally he poured himself another stiff jolt of rye whiskey, slapped the cork into the bottle with the palm of his hand and stood up, ready to turn in for the night. Then he stood, stiff and wary, as his ears picked up the tinkle of a spur outside the door. The door opened and the lank, thin figure of Hitch Wheeler pushed through. Quarney grunted and relaxed.

"Why don't you knock?" he rapped acidly.

Hitch Wheeler showed his twisted, sardonic grin. "That's for others, not for me. What kind of crooked business you and Broderick been cooking up?"

A faint flush stained Quarney's gaunt cheeks. "That's no way to talk to me."

Hitch Wheeler shrugged. "I know you, and I know Broderick. Not an honest bone in the body of either of you. Facts are facts, even though unpleasant. That's a lesson I learned a long time ago. You taught it to me. You told me about facts."

The flush in Quarney's cheeks deepened. "What are you here for?"

Wheeler leaned over, took a handful of cigars from the box and tucked them into a shirt pocket. "Some more facts. Man has to eat to live and it costs money to eat."

"Just how long do you think you can go on bleeding me?" snapped Quarney. "I'm getting tired of it."

Wheeler did not answer right away. He picked up the whiskey bottle, shook it, eyed its contents against the lamplight. He pulled the cork, tipped the bottle at his lips, swallowed a couple of times, and then smacked his lips.

"Best quality rye," he said, putting back the bottle cork. "Do right well by yourself, don't you, Mister Quarney? Always have, for that matter. High-class whiskey, high-class cigars. Yet you whine over the few dollars you hand out to me. Wouldn't be selfish, would you?"

Hitch Wheeler straightened, looked straight at Mike Quarney, a certain bitter chill in his eyes. Quarney tried to meet the glance, couldn't do it, cursed softly and reached inside his coat for his billfold. He laid several bills on the table.

"There's fifty dollars. Don't come around for any more. You won't get it — unless —." Quarney paused, as though struck with a sudden thought.

"Unless what?" prompted Wheeler.

Quarney looked at him. "You prowl the country a great deal. You see men riding.

They tell me you're sharp with a gun. Now if you should see a certain man riding and did a quick, good job of it with a gun, there could be a lot more than fifty dollars in it for you."

"How much more?"

"Five — ten times as much."

Wheeler laughed softly. "I figured the only man you hated that bad was Dan Brandon, because he was the one who had most to do with kicking the spokes out of your political wheel and making you an ex-senator. But Brandon's dead. Who is this other fellow you'd pay five hundred dollars to see in the same shape?"

The taunt and sarcasm in Hitch Wheeler's voice and words pulled Quarney's cheeks rigid. He managed to keep his anger bottled.

"Before I name him — are you really interested?"

"Five hundred dollars are enough to interest any man. Who?"

"Leach Carlin."

Wheeler was very still for a moment, his face turning unreadable, his eyes shadowed. He spoke slowly. "You don't pick 'em easy, do you? That fellow's no slouch with a gun himself. I might miss and he wouldn't."

Quarney shrugged. "You just said five

hundred was a lot. Well, it's yours if Carlin is found dead along some trail."

Hitch Wheeler gathered up the money on the table, pocketed it. He turned to the door and spoke over his shoulder, his narrow face still inscrutable.

"You're the only full-blooded coyote I ever saw with only two legs, Mister Quarney. That five hundred dollars? I'll collect it — and more!"

The door closed and Quarney stood alone. His lips twisted in a burst of low, furious cursing and his words ran thickly vicious. "I hope you do miss — and that Carlin connects!"

CHAPTER FOUR

For a couple of days, Leach Carlin did not get over a half mile from Hackamore headquarters. He spent considerable time with Martha Brandon while she supplied him with the fabric of plans, so far as she was able, which Dan Brandon had discussed with her for the immediate future. Then he talked with various members of the crew, getting their reactions to the current ranch business and their ideas of what needed to be done. Gradually he began to pick up the feel of the ranch again.

Always there was that growing and sobering sense of complete responsibility. It was all his, now. Before, the major responsibilities had reposed with Brandon. As foreman, he had merely to carry out orders, to translate them into action and results. If one such order turned out to be the wrong one, the fault was not his, but Brandon's. Now, however, all the weight was on him alone.

Joe Spence and Jimmy Spurlock had shown up as they promised, had taken bunks and were again part and parcel of the

Hackamore crew. Carlin drew Joe Spence aside.

"When I'm not around, Joe — you're in charge."

"Me!" Startled, Joe stared at him. "Hell, man — I'm just a forty-and-found cowhand. I can take orders, but I can't give 'em."

"You've never tried. You'll learn. Just follow your common sense — you've plenty of that. You know cattle and you know ranch work. With no more equipment than that, men have built empires."

Joe thumbed his hat to the back of his grizzled head, scrubbed a worried palm across his chin. "There's Clint," he reminded. "Him and me are sure to tangle."

"You leave Clint to me," said Carlin. "If he tries to argue, stick to your guns. Call things exactly as you see them. You'll do all right."

Leathery old Joe gave a mock groan. "Was it anybody else but you, Leach — ! Well, I'll give it a whirl and we'll see."

The rest of the crew took the word without rancor or jealousy. A new order of things had come to Hackamore and they knew full well which way the wind blew.

Around mid-afternoon of the second day, Sam and Beth Desmond rode up in a buckboard. Carlin went over to the rig, touched his hat to Beth. "Light down, folks. Like old times, having you drop in."

Beth, as usual, was striking in her dark beauty. She knew how to wear clothes, this girl did. No matter what she wore, she wore it with a flair. Right now she had on a khaki blouse and divided skirt, and many women in satin would have been far less attractive. She stepped from the buckboard and held out her hand.

"It seems congratulations are in order, Leach." There was a pressure in her slim fingers.

"Thanks. Hope I'm big enough for the job."

"Mrs. Brandon seems to think you are. That makes two of us." She glanced toward the ranch house. "I'm wondering if she'd rather be alone?"

"Go right on in," advised Carlin. "Company is what she needs most of, just now. She has a great loneliness to fight."

Carlin watched Beth until the ranch-house door closed behind her, then turned to find Sam Desmond surveying him with a troubled, speculative glance.

"Know where Clint is?" Desmond asked.

Carlin shook his head. "Haven't seen him for the best part of two days."

"He's in town," stated Desmond. "And

hitting the bottle. What's got into him?"

Carlin's glance was very direct. "I guess you know, Sam. The new setup here doesn't please him a bit. But he's a fool if he's taking his mad out on a whiskey bottle."

Sam Desmond looked away. "Can't blame him too much. It was natural for him to believe he'd take over here. Bound to be a big disappointment to find out different. I'm wondering —."

"What are you wondering, Sam?"

A slight flush touched Sam Desmond's loose features. "Wondering if Martha Brandon's judgment in this is entirely right. Oh, no reflection on you, understand. I don't know where she could have found a better man for the job. But I'm thinking of Clint, too. Sure, he's had it pretty soft all his life, maybe too soft. And in some ways it hasn't done him a bit of good. But you never know just how tall a man might measure, until you give him a chance. It could be that full responsibility for Hackamore would have brought out a lot of worth-while things in Clint."

Carlin kept his tone level. "I wouldn't know about that, Sam. Mrs. Brandon must have had her own good reasons for asking me to take over. I'm not going to question them. And until she says different, that's the way it will be."

"Oh, sure, sure," said Desmond hurriedly. "I know you'll do a job of it."

A couple of the Hackamore crew were working at some odd chores around the feed sheds and Desmond headed that way to gossip with them. Carlin watched him go, marking the loose, lunging walk, the lumpy sagging shoulders. It was plain that Sam Desmond didn't like the new order at Hackamore, didn't like it a bit. Not that it was really any of his business. But — why?

Maybe, thought Carlin, because Sam figured Clint would be easier to sponge on. Maybe it went further than that. Thinking back on how Beth Desmond and Clint had been more and more together over the past year or two, and with Sam's full approval, maybe Sam had been hoping that Beth and Clint would make a match of it, thus making Sam's future more secure.

Carlin swung his shoulders restlessly, and in some moodiness of spirit crossed over and let himself into the office. He considered the word Desmond had given him about Clint. He hadn't seen Clint since that first night, when Clint stood on the bunkhouse step, hating him. And he'd wondered at Clint's absence, since.

So Clint was in town, riding the whiskey route. Well, it wasn't surprising. It gave a pretty good estimate of Clint's real measure of strength — or the lack of it. There were some who were like that, looking to the bottle when things went against them.

Carlin knew a quick gust of anger. Damn Clint, anyhow! By hitting the bottle he'd be hurting his mother far more than himself. And not caring a damn, of course, in his selfishness and self-pity.

Building a smoke, Carlin considered the future and with a deep pang of regret knew what that future certainly portended. Clint was due to hurt Martha Brandon in many ways.

Carlin sat down at the desk, began checking off a list of things already done and considering others still to do; little items of slack that had crept into the ranch affairs during the final weeks of Brandon's fading strength. A ranch, mused Carlin, was like that. It moved only to the pace and purpose of the guiding hand behind it. Take the push of that hand away, even for a little time, and an inevitable inertia began to show itself.

A half hour slipped by and then the inner door of the office opened and Beth Desmond came in. She perched on a corner of the desk and looked down at Carlin.

"Dad tell you about Clint?" she asked abruptly.

Carlin nodded. "Might be a good way for him to get it all out of his system. He'll have a sore head to remind him."

"It won't solve anything, not with Clint. Why does a man have to be such a fool?"

Carlin rounded up another cigarette. "Certain amount of fool in all men, I reckon. Some show it one way, some in another."

"How does it show up in you, Leach?"

He met her dark-eyed glance, held it until a shade of confusion ripened her cheeks. "Hard question to answer," he fenced carefully. "Guess I've been such in lots of ways." He considered a moment, then added, "A man's never hopeless though, if he learns as he goes along."

"That," stated Beth, "has a kind of left-handed sound to it."

He showed her a faint grin. "Best I can do."

She slid off the desk, took a short turn up and down the room, came to a stop beside his chair. "We used to be pretty good friends, Leach — you and me."

There was subtle challenge in the way she stood, in her proximity, in the shadowed sultriness of her eyes. Carlin came abruptly to his feet, caught her by the shoulders, squared her around to face him fully. The shadow of a smile touched her lips and she leaned toward him, but stopped this move halfway when his voice hit her with a startling harshness.

"Beth, I want a good look at you!"

She did her best to meet and hold the fixed intensity of his searching glance. A strange fear stirred up within her, for she had the uneasy conviction that for the first time in her life a man was seeing completely through her, seeing her inner self and into the last guarded recess of her mind. It was as though she were being stripped, mentally. She tried to erect some kind of barrier, but couldn't. The half smile left her lips and a certain slackness took its place. Her eyes slid away.

Carlin let go of her, stepped past her. She tried to pass the moment off with a shaky laugh. "Well, you certainly had your look. What did you see?"

Carlin's answer was curt. "Just — Beth Desmond." He moved to the outer door. The line of his jaw was bleak.

She tried to hold things together. "Mrs. Brandon wants Dad and me to stay to supper. You'll sit in, Leach?"

He shook his head, his tone going casual

again. "I'm for town. Somebody has to go drag Clint away from that bottle before he begins finding snakes in his pockets."

She pouted a little over this, then tipped a softly rounded shoulder in discontent. "Perhaps it's just as well. You're a strange man, my friend."

He considered, then said, as he opened the door, "Maybe. But not twice the fool in the same way."

Carlin barely beat sunset into town. He went directly to the Skyhigh, but found the place empty except for Ace Lanier behind the bar. Ace started to set out bottle and glass, but Carlin shook his head.

"Looking for Clint. Where is he, Ace?"

Ace replied, somewhat waspishly, "Damned if I know — or care. Just so he don't bother me any more. What a souse! One of the mouthy kind. Feels sorry for himself. My God — how sorry! I finally ran him out."

"Did you have to let him have so much, Ace?"

Ace Lanier spread both hands on top of the bar. He was a thick-set man with a twisted nose, relic of some ancient barroom brawl, and there was no fear him.

"Man grown, ain't he? Don't blame me if he don't know his own liquor limit."

"Sure," nodded Carlin, turning for the door. "Forget it."

Ace's tone went friendly again as he called after Carlin.

"He seems like to choke to death on the hate he packs for you, Leach. So why worry about him?"

Out in the street again, Carlin's glance swung left and right, searching the hitch rails. Then he shook his head. Clint had been in town two days and two nights. Even had he neglected his horse and left it at a hitch rail, Coony Fyle would have taken care of the animal. Coony was that way. Any time a careless rider left his mount on the street longer than Coony thought it should be there, untended, Coony would take the animal to his stable, care for it, and then take his pay when the rider came to claim the mount, by giving the rider a good tongue-lashing. Coony Fyle was a good man.

Carlin went down street to the stable and met Coony and Doc Persall just coming out of the place. Doc had his battered kit bag in his hand.

"If you're looking for Clint," Doc said, "he's inside. And sick as a pig. Damn fool! What got into him, anyhow?"

Carlin shrugged. "Ace Lanier said he was feeling sorry for himself."

"Then he's the only one," said Doc acidly. "About two more drinks of that sorrow and he'd have been combIng centipedes out of his hair." Doc stamped off up street.

Carlin built a cigarette. "You haul him in, Coony?"

Coony nodded. "Took his horse in yesterday, then him today. He was a mess. Me and Doe sluiced him off and put him under a blanket." Coony spat in disgust.

Carlin put a hand in his pocket, but Coony shook a quick head. "None of it was for pay, Leach. Not for Clint, either. But for Mrs. Brandon."

Carlin dropped a hand on Coony's shoulder. "Get back at you some way. Thanks."

The stage from Centerville, forty miles back across the Warners, came creaking and rocking into town, pulled up at Billy Prior's store long enough to drop off a mailbag, then came on down to the stable, the sweating team moving at a weary, shuffling walk. Swing Benson, the whip, tossed his reins down to Coony Fyle and then climbed slowly down himself. He stretched and shook his shoulders, stirring away a faint blur of dust.

"Road seems longer every trip. Mebbe it's me, getting older by the day. Leach, how are you?"

"Good enough, Swing. Any mail for

Hackamore in that sack you just got rid of?"

"Could be. Little fatter than usual."

Benson and Coony Fyle began unhooking the stage team. Carlin headed for the store. Billy Prior had just emptied the mail sack on his counter and, under the evening's first glow of a big hanging lamp, started sorting it. Lyle Barnard, the banker, stood watching him. Barnard looked up as Carlin entered, nodded.

"Evening, Leach. Been thinking about you, how you stand as the start of a new era in these parts."

Carlin, puzzled, frowned. "Don't exactly get you, Lyle."

Barnard chuckled. "Couple of Hackamore checks came through, signed by you. After so many years of seeing Dan Brandon's scrawl, it takes a bit of getting used to."

Up street the hotel supper gong jangled mellowly. "I'll buy your supper, Leach," said Barnard. "Want to talk to you." He turned to the storekeeper. "How you coming, Billy?"

"All right, Lyle. Here's yours." Prior handed a small packet of mail to the banker. "Sorry, Leach — nothing for Hackamore."

Steps sounded at the doorway and Mike Quarney came in, tall and gaunt in his loose, black, knee-length coat. The lamplight, cutting in at sharp angles under the wide brim of his black hat, built a raw sharpness about his beaked face. His glance was a mere flicker touching Carlin and Barnard, his nod barely perceptible.

"Gentlemen!" he murmured. Then he looked at Billy Prior. "Anything for me?"

Carlin and Barnard went out into the street and the banker spoke. "A very self-contained man, Leach." He pondered a moment, then added dryly, "I mistrust such."

Carlin tipped a swift glance. "How so, Lyle?"

Barnard shrugged. "Maybe a purely personal conception, understand. Yet I like to see a gleam of fellowship in a man's eye, and a willingness to occasional laughter. Quarney is the sort to nurse a hate to his deathbed."

"Nothing for him to hate now," observed Carlin briefly. "Dan Brandon is dead."

"Regretfully true. But that which Brandon built, Hackamore, is still a live and going concern. I'd keep an eye on Mister Quarney, Leach."

They went along a street that was filling with the soft, blue push of cool autumn dusk. The hush of day's end lay over the land and in the motionless poplar trees some sparrows had set up their evening cheeping, a drowsy, peaceful sound.

They climbed the steps of the hotel, crossed the porch and went through the foyer to the dining room. They took a side table and ordered up their meal. Carlin looked across at his companion. "What was it you wanted to talk about, Lyle?"

"Clint — and Hackamore," said Barnard slowly. "Clint first. Where and how is he going to fit in with the new order of things out at the ranch? How are you going to get along with him?"

"Just curiosity, Lyle — or business?"

"Both," admitted the banker frankly. "Hackamore is one of my best accounts. Naturally I want to see it grow and prosper. Even the most generous of us, after observing the kind of fool Clint's been making of himself for the past day or two, would have to admit that Hackamore, under his management, would be in for dark days. So I'm wondering how much Clint is going to have to say about the ranch's affairs?"

Carlin was silent for a moment, then answered thoughtfully, "For the present, nothing. The future, as always, is something no man can call exactly. Put it this way. While I keep my good health, Clint will just have to play second fiddle."

Lyle Barnard looked at him sharply. "I see no good reason to doubt your health."

Carlin showed a hint of a bleak smile. "Man never knows. One thing is sure — I'll have my enemies."

The banker sat for a time in thought, tapping the table with his fingers. He was a neat, incisive man, pleasant and approachable, beginning to gray a little at the temples.

"Let's be realistic about this, Leach. It's easy to understand why Martha, in the momentary helplessness of grief and loss, should seek a strong shoulder to lean on — yours, as a matter of fact. But as time passes, being a mother, it seems only natural to me that she should begln to consider Clint more and more and, perhaps, turn the ranch over to him. Mothers are that way toward sons, you know. Time won't change Clint, though. He'll always be — Clint. And should he ever take over, Hackamore would certainly come apart at the seams."

"I'm not going to try and guess at the future," said Carlin slowly. "I'm just going to take each day as it comes and hope for the best."

Mike Quarney came into the dining room, took a corner table to himself and buried himself in a periodical of some sort that had come to him through the mail. Lyle Barnard's words were murmur soft.

"Ex-servant of the people. Fooled those people for a long time, too. But never Dan Brandon, who was a canny man in such things. So Dan led the move which retired the gentleman yonder to private life. I'm saying again, keep an eye on Quarney, Leach. For politics can breed some lasting and savage hates. Also, there's a mean streak in Quarney. He's just the sort to never forget and never forgive, and, if he can't hit directly back at a man because that man is dead, then he'll take it out on the man's family. Shrewd enough, too, to turn that hate into a profit, if he can get away with it. Yes, Leach — with the responsibility of Hackamore all yours, now — you watch him."

Carlin smiled grimly. "You certainly have definite ideas in the matter, Lyle."

"My business," retorted the banker cheerfully, "to have definite ideas on people and affairs."

They finished their meal and on the way out the banker produced cigars. They lighted up, stood for a moment on the porch, savoring the good smoke.

"Probably be a gentleman's game at the Skyhigh later on," observed Barnard. "Now if you should drop around, I'd enjoy separating you from a dollar or two of your hard-earned money."

Carlin chuckled. "My friend, you're too proud. I'll probably be there."

On coming to town, Carlin's plan had been to get hold of Clint and take him back to the ranch right away. But with Clint now sleeping it off in Coony Fyle's harness room, there was nothing to do but wait it out for morning. Which Carlin now decided to do. So he collected his horse and led it down to the stable.

Night was fully down, now, and the chill of it had come in from the heights of the Warners. Doors all along the street were closed and windows gave forth their light in short, yellow lances which started boldly into the dark, then frittered out with abrupt caution. A great horned owl, on the hunt from its daylight covert in some far, timbered mountain canyon, now perched in one of the poplar trees along the street and hollowly boomed its challenge.

At the stable, Coony Fyle was not around, so Carlin took care of his horse himself. Passing the harness room on the way out, he could hear Clint's sodden snores. The sound drove a sharp gust of anger through him.

At the Skyhigh the evening game was about to start. Swing Benson, the stage whip, was there, and Doc Persall. Hoot McLean had drifted into town in the interval and was claiming a chair. A little later Billy Prior, having locked up for the night, came over from his store. Then Lyle Barnard showed and with Carlin this filled the table and they settled back to enjoy a couple of hours.

This was a friendly game, a low-limit one, and good-natured comment besides cards, went back and forth across the table. At intervals, when his bar was empty, Ace Lanier drifted over to watch and add a comfortable remark every now and then.

Mike Quarney came in, stayed at the bar over a couple of drinks, then, glass in hand, moved up to watch. Betting a pair of nines with a confidence that suggested a third one in the hole, Carlin made Doc Persall take water when Doc had him beat on sight with a pair of queens. Mike Quarney spoke thinly.

"You run a pretty good bluff, Carlin."

Carlin twisted his head, looked up. "Sometimes," he said briefly. "Not always."

"That's right," said Doc Persall ruefully. "Over this damn table I've paid Leach often enough to have found that out. Trouble is, just when you think he hasn't got 'em — he has."

For a short moment Carlin's and Quarney's eyes held, Quarney's shadowed and expressionless, Carlin's cool and equally un-readable. Quarney downed the rest of his drink and moved away. A little later he left.

The game ran along quietly. Doc Persall filled a low straight on his last card and nipped Carlin, who was backing two big pair. Doc chuckled his satisfaction and ordered up a drink all around.

At eleven o'clock the door swung and Carlin looked up to see Clint come in. He was blear-eyed, frowsy, and dirty, but fairly sober again. Ace Lanier looked at him with a vast distaste, then swung his head to glance at Carlin, who held up one finger. Ace nodded and poured the drink. Clint gulped it and shoved the glass across for another. Ace shook his head.

"That's all for tonight."

Clint considered this, looked at Carlin with blood-shot eyes, turned and went out. Ace scrubbed his bar with extra vehemence. Doc Persall sighed. "What's the use? You'll have a fine job getting him home tonight in that shape, Leach."

Carlin pushed in his cards and got to his feet. "Not going to try. I'll make a night of it in Pee Dee Kyne's hotel."

He went out into the night, stood listening for a time and heard Clint shuffling back toward the stable. He followed along until he was sure Clint had turned in there, then went back to the Skyhigh. The game had broken up and Lyle Barnard was treating all to a nightcap.

Doc Persall said, "I should have stuck a needle into him, Leach, and knocked him cold for about twelve hours."

Carlin said, "He'll keep, Doc. He's gone back to the stable."

Carlin went over to the hotel with Lyle Barnard. Pee Dee Kyne had already turned in for the night, so Carlin crossed to the desk, signed for a small, second-story room he'd used a number of times in the past, said good night to Barnard, then climbed the stairs. He yawned sleepily as he undressed and turned in.

For a little time, thought held him drowsily. He mused over the swiftness with which a man's fortunes could change. Just a few short days ago he'd come in out of the mountains, with the future only something to guess at. Now he was in charge of Hackamore, biggest ranch on the prairie. And faced with a future certain to hold its troubles, large and small.

Well, he'd gone into it with his eyes open. The request had been Martha Brandon's, but the acceptance his own. On that he'd ride. He burrowed his head deeper into the pillow and went to sleep.

Somewhere in the small hours of the morning he awoke. He lay for a moment, wondering why, for his conscience was clear and his state of health sound. Then he heard it, a faint slither of sound that told him he wasn't alone in the room.

The instinct that had awakened him now sharpened to a razor edge, and his thoughts broke keen and clear out of a fog of sleep. He kept up the slow, even cadence of his breathing, as though still asleep. He lay partly on his right side, partly on his back. This put him more or less facing the open window, with the door of the room at his back. The cold gleam of late stars beamed a faint radiance beyond the window, but no hint of that light penetrated the room. Carlin knew he'd be able to see nothing, even if he turned his head, and that could be a betraying move.

On turning in, he'd hung his belt and gun on the foot of the bed. It would take movement and time to get clear of the blankets and grab for the gun and get it free. He had to play this thing out a little longer and gamble on what he could hear.

The movement was there, all right, the small faintness of sound that came up when the pressure of a stealthy step was placed on the floor. And breathing, human breathing, short and guarded. Then the faintest sound of impact against the side of the bed, as someone touched it and leaned over.

That sharpening instinct in Carlin became a noiseless shout. He threw his left arm up and over, driving the folds of the blankets ahead of it. With the same move he rolled to the right, lunging clear of the bed.

He felt the blow come down, on that upflung, blanket-swathed left arm, heard the sharp exhalation of breath behind the effort. And he felt a slicing burn across his left forearm. Then, impact against the floor shook him.

He rolled over, got his feet under him and drove for the foot of the bed and his gun. It took him a fumbling moment to get at the weapon and before he could manage it there was a rush of movement and then he was alone in the room again.

Gun in fist, Carlin drove for the door, but even as he made the hall he could hear running steps already clattering down the stairs to the floor below and he knew that pursuit would do him no good. He whirled back to the window of his room, peered out and down at the street's cold blackness. He thought he caught a glimpse of someone breaking clear of the far end of the hotel porch, but he couldn't be certain, and the dark swallowed any further movement. So he turned back, held for a moment in a gust of savage, wicked anger.

The sting of pain on his left forearm and the warm, sticky moistness there, brought him back to earth. He tossed his gun on the bed, located his shirt, got a match from a pocket and lit the small lamp on the battered old bureau which stood in the wall angle by the window.

Now he could hear movement downstairs and then the slap-slap of slippered feet climbing the stairs. A moment later the pinched, gnome-like face of Pee Dee Kyne peered in at Carlin's door.

"What's the fuss — what's the fuss?" demanded the little hotel owner with sleepy peevishness. "Did I hear somebody leaving at a run?"

"You did, Pee Dee," said Carlin, his voice quiet, but carrying a bitter ring of harshness. "How's chances for a pitcher of water and cloth enough for a bandage?"

Pee Dee stared. "Hell, man — you're bleeding!"

"A little. Somebody tried to stick a knife in me. There's a rip in a couple of your blankets, and some blood smeared. There'll be more of it if you don't rustle up that

111

water and a bandage."

"Be damned!" exclaimed Pee Dee, and slap-slapped away.

Carlin waited stoically for Pee Dee's return and while he did so became aware of something else in the room which, up to now, he'd missed. It was the smell of whiskey, second-hand and strong, which the intruder had brought with him and left behind. As he considered the implications of this, Carlin's jaw was coldly rigid; and his eyes were burning with a deep flame when, a little later, Pee Dee returned, to watch Carlin wash his wound and help him bandage it.

It was in no way serious, a shallow, slicing cut across the heavy forearm muscles, more an inconvenience for a time than anything else, now that the bleeding was staunched and a bandage securely in place. But Pee Dee was bursting with questions. He was a cricket of a man, with the probing curiosity of a jay bird.

"Who was it, Leach?"

Carlin shrugged. "You guess, Pee Dee."

"But why?" demanded Pee Dee. "Why would anybody want to stick a knife into you?"

Carlin laughed mirthlessly. "I guess they just don't like me."

He got out the makings and built a cigarette without too much trouble. He looked at Pee Dee through the smoke of it, his eyes still dark with the congealed anger in him. "You can be garrulous as a crow at times, Pee Dee. But not this time. You're keeping this whole thing under your hat. Not a peep to anybody — savvy? As a favor to me."

"Sure, Leach — sure." Pee Dee bobbed his head. "But that dirty son-of-a-gun, trying to knife one of my folks, right here in my own hotel! If I'd 'a caught him at it, I'd 'a shotgunned him."

"That goes for both of us," said Carlin. "Now rustle yourself back to bed and like I said — forget it. Thanks for helping."

Pee Dee went out, still muttering wrathfully.

Carlin went to the window again, surveyed the street. Things were a little more distinct; where complete blackness had been before, there was now a growing grayness. Dawn was not too far away.

Carlin got into his clothes, left the hotel qnletly, went down street to Coony Fyle's stable. In here it was still deep dark, but Carlin was familiar enough with the place to find his way around. He listened at the door of the harness room, but found no sound of any kind in there, except the faint squeak and scurry of a mouse. Carlin scratched a match and made a quick survey. Clint was gone.

Carlin went deeper into the stable, feeling his way along, his senses sharp and penetrating. Horses already busily munching at their morning's feeding filled the place with a faint warmth. One of them, sensing Carlin's presence, whickered softly at him.

Satisfied at length that no humans were about the place, Carlin went back to the street and turned toward the hotel. Way out east beyond the Nevada Hills the horizon was cut clearly against a slash of silver and rose, and birds were wakening in the trees along the street.

Carlin climbed to his room, smoothed the rumpled bed and lay back on it. The wounded arm was a small discomfort, soon forgotten in the heavy timbre of his thoughts. So he rested, watching day's light grow and brighten beyond the window.

CHAPTER FIVE

"I don't know what time Clint pulled out, Leach," said Coony Fyle. "I figured he was set for the night, the way he was snoring the last time I looked in on him. But when I came to do my chores this morning, there wasn't hide or hair of him anywhere. His bronc and gear were gone, too. Guess he must have sobered up and decided to cut for home. Something wrong with your arm? You're handling it kind of easy."

Leach Carlin, engaged in saddling up, put his back to the sharp-eyed Coony. "An old sprain," he said briefly. "Comes back to bother me now and then."

Carlin had breakfasted early at the hotel. Now in the saddle, he kept to the home trail only a little way before turning off at an angle, heading out across the miles toward the Indian Mounds. For two reasons.

First, he didn't want to face Clint just yet, not until he'd at least softened to some extent the moil of anger which still lingered dark and cold in him. And he wanted a look at the stretch of range which Case Broderick had given his ultimatum on. He wanted to see if the blunt answer he'd handed Broderick had meant anything, or if Broderick was making any move toward doing what he'd threatened — which was to move in. There was only one way to know for sure, and that was to go and see.

His route took him well out toward the middle of Big Sage Prairie, where the river wound and pushed its way along to where the Warners and the Nevada Hills pulled together in a notch, made blue and misted by distance, the beginnings of a rock-ribbed gorge which compressed the river waters into wild, white-laced turbulence before finally letting them flow free again. Beyond those pressed-in ramparts lay a wide plains country. Granger country, and a country of fences and plowed fields.

An hour's steady jogging brought Carlin within sight of Bois Renfro's small, two-man layout, and in sudden decision he headed there. He'd always liked Bois Renfro. There was a rugged solidity and a blunt honesty about the man which made others seek his friendship and value it.

Here, closer to the river, Carlin began seeing cattle in the side draws and along the warmed slopes of the low, billowing earth swells, which disproved the all-over illusion that Big Sage was an utterly flat country. Some of the cattle were Hackamore, some Renfro's Sawbuck. They were, Carlin noted mechanically, in good condition, which meant that they would winter well.

Moving in on Sawbuck headquarters, Carlin heard the clatter of a hammer and saw Bois Renfro and his lone ranch hand, Barney Welch, up on the roof of the ranch house, setting some new shakes in place. Renfro grinned down at Carlin and his big voice rumbled.

"Got to do this to keep my womenfolks home. They both swore they wouldn't put in another winter in this house unless I made sure there'd be no leaks. Free advice to you, Leach. Never let a woman get where she can boss you. You do, you'll say good-by to peace forever."

Dallas Renfro stepped from the ranch house door. "That's right, Leach. Listen to him. Nothing so dangerous as a designing woman."

"I wonder," drawled Carlin, meeting her smile.

She was reed-slender, with the same easy grace and pliable, bending strength. A cheerful, sunny girl, full of clear laughter, loving life and all that it held. Looking at her, some of the dregs of his dark anger left him.

117

"I'm riding a little jaunt down past the Indian Mounds," he said. "It'd be a lot more interesting ride if I had one of these dangerous women along. Well?"

"Love it!" she exclaimed. "I need a change of company. Dad's full of grumbles and Barney can never think of anything to talk about. Mother's making up her winter's mincemeat and when she does, she never wants anyone around to bother her. Just give me time to change." She whisked back into the house.

Up on the roof, Bois Renfro got out a stubby pipe, packed and lit it, puffed a reflective moment. Then he squinted down at Carlin shrewdly.

"As boss of Hackamore, you got other things to do besides ram around on a horse, just for the hell of it. What's so interesting down at the Indian Mounds?"

Carlin considered a moment, then told of Broderick's statement of intentions concerning the range tween the Indian Mounds and Steptoe Creek. Renfro snorted.

"Got his gall, ain't he? And as much right to that range as I have, which is none at all. Doesn't make him shape up any bigger as a man, either — coming at Martha that way so soon after old Dan died. I can imagine the answer he got."

Carlin nodded. "He was told. But you know, Bois, on thinking on it, I can't see why Dan Brandon ever went to the bother of putting his hand on that range in the first place. It's not connected in any way with the main Hackamore holdings, but way off by itself. And not what you'd call good cattle country, either."

"Wondered about that a couple of times myself," Renfro admitted. "But old Dan was a shrewd one. He always had a pretty good reason for anything he did in a business way, so I reckon he must have had one there."

"That's why I want another look at the range," said Carlin. "Could be something there I never noticed the other times I've ridden across it."

Carlin went over to the corrals, shook out his rope and caught up a compact, quick-stepping buckskin which he recalled as Dallas Renfro's favorite mount. He had the animal saddled and waiting by the time Dallas came hurrying over, hat in hand, a crimson scarf about her throat giving a bright touch of color to the neutral-shaded blouse and divided skirt she wore. As she swung into the saddle she threw a smiling jibe.

"The man's fairly human, at least. He remembers my pet horse."

"You'd be surprised the things I remember," retorted Carlin. "Like a dance one time in the loft of Billy Prior's warehouse, and a walk in the moonlight afterward."

She colored, but did not flinch. "And," she supplied lightly, "the moonlight addled you and you kissed me, and then spoiled it all by apologizing all over the place. Probably," she added, tartly sweet, "because you felt you hadn't been true to Beth Desmond. You didn't fool me a bit, my fine friend."

Carlin shook his head ruefully. "Your father's right. A man can't win."

They broke down to the river flats and rode on south along them. The signs of the season were at hand. The solid green of the willow clumps showed yellowish tones here and there, and some scrub alders had a partly clothed look where the lower leaves had shed. From several of the larger river pools, gusts of wild mallard ducks spouted suddenly up in a flurry of beating wings, the heads of the drakes glinting a brliliant, metallic green.

Several coveys of quail buzzed away and then, from the thickets where they settled again, called poignantly. At one shallows a little band of antelope, startled from their drinking, scudded away, shadow swift, the white alarm hairs on their rumps glinting in the morning sun as they breasted the short upslope that lifted them to the main roll of the prairie. And once, from some far height, the call of geese winging south was like the echo of some great, distant clarion. Dallas, missing none of this, spoke abruptly.

"The sad season approaches, and it gives me the melancholies."

Carlin looked at her, showed a small smile. "Hard to please, that's you. Now me, I figure the Lord did a great job in making the four seasons. Keeps a man's soul from shriveling up from too much monotony. Now what would the aspens be like if they didn't turn gold in the fall?"

"I know," she said, with a simple wistfulness that was strangely appealing. "You're right, of course. But I don't like winter. It can be cruel, and I don't like cruelty. Now if we could jump from fall to spring, that would be wonderful."

"Too big a jump," said Carlin dryly. "World ain't built that way. Might as well take things as they are and like them."

Her mood changed and she jeered at him with the old bright mischief. "Senor Philosopher himself. Tell me, how's the new job going? The weight of it doesn't seem to have bowed your shoulders any."

"Give it a little time. Chances are a year from now it'll have me wore plumb down to a nubbin. Full of miseries and crotchety as an old mule."

She tipped her head as she surveyed him. "Somehow I can't see you that way. The original hard rock, that's you. You're the kind that wears well."

He grinned. "As a husband, do you think?"

She tossed her head. "A completely uninteresting subject. Managing a stubborn father is chore enough for me."

Carlin's left arm was aching a little and he favored it cautiously, but not cautiously enough to evade this girl's alert glance.

"What's the matter with your arm, Leach?" Then, accusingly, "You've been fighting again."

He edged away from her primary question. "My reputation that bad?"

"I didn't ask about your reputation, sir — I asked about your arm. Why are you favoring it?"

He gave her the same answer he'd given Coony Fyle and she sniffed her open disbelief. "Stick to the truth, my friend. You'll never be a success at trying to avoid it. But of course, if you don't want to tell —."

Carlin's answer was his silence.

For the past several miles they had been riding down a steadily descending slope of country, for here the long run of Big Sage

Prairie broke steadily toward lower ground, funneling toward the river gap, and narrowing as the Warners and the Nevada Hills began to push in from either side. The country was broken with side gulches and winding ridges which reached in and out. Stands of timber crested some of the ridges and the gulches were brush choked. And always the course of the river dropped lower and lower and the speeding water seemed to be gathering energy for the battle with the constricting gorge walls there at the misty gap ahead.

Here also Indian Mounds lifted, a pair of almost identical earth bulges, swelling smooth and rounded, a couple of hundred feet high from base to crest. They stood some three hundred yards apart and the river between them, dodging through a tunnel of alders.

Some half mile beyond the Indian Mounds, Carlin put his horse to the climb up the point of a side ridge and on reaching this eminence he reined in, sagged sideways in his saddle and spun up a smoke, his eyes roving the country below and ahead.

A few cattle were in evidence, a couple flushing close enough for him to read the Hackamore brand. Those brushed-up side gulches would hold more, he decided, and it would be the devil's own chore to chouse them into the clear. Even the ones he had glimpsed were wild and wary as deer. Pulled up beside Carlin, Dallas Renfro spoke.

"Back home, the window of my room was open, so I heard what you told Dad about Case Broderick claiming this piece of range. I can't see why he would want it, or why Dan Brandon ever claimed it. Look how wild those cattle are, Leach. I'll bet those brushy side draws are full of mavericks that will never wear a brand unless somebody is fool enough to put in more time and effort working them than the critters are worth."

Carlin glanced at her. The ride had done things for her, putting a glow in her softly browned cheeks. In repose her lips were sweetly curved and her chin carried a little tilt to it.

"Shrewd one, you," he said. "You've voiced my own thoughts. I can't see any real value to this stretch for anyone."

"Then," she said quickly, "why not let Broderick have it and be done with it?"

Carlin drew a deep inhale of smoke, crushed the butt of his cigarette on his saddle horn. "Several reasons — all good. First, because it is Broderick. Second, because of the way he went at demanding it.

Third, because he's a liar — Dan Brandon didn't hog the range from him. Fourth, because if Hackamore let Broderick get by with one bite, then he and probably others would think that Hackamore was turning soft and easy, so they'd start gnawing away at the really good Hackamore range further up the prairie. That enough reasons?"

"I suppose. But I bet I can add a fifth. Men! Just men. Proud, stiff-necked critters. Like little boys. Trying to shoulder each other back and forth across a line in the dust of the street. And ending up in a fight. Over what? Nothing that really counts."

Carlin grinned. "Are we really that bad — us men?"

"Worse!" She met his glance and her manner sobered. "Understand me right, Leach. I think Martha Brandon is a wonderful woman and I love her, I truly do. I can also understand why she should like to keep Hackamore just as it was before Dan Brandon died. But I don't like the position you've been placed in."

Carlin's glance became a little more intent. "How's that?"

Her soft chin stole out a little further. "Dan Brandon was a good man, I guess. But he had a way about him that made him a lot of enemies. Which was his own affair, so long as he was alive to fight his own battles. But I don't like to see you placed in a position where you have to carry on the quarrels he started. It's not fair to you."

She met his eyes and held them very steadily, though she couldn't keep a betraying warmth from her cheeks. She gave her head a little toss. "It's my opinion, Leach — and I've a right to it."

Carlin's voice ran gentle. "Bless your heart, of course you have. You're quite a person, Dallas. You really are. Thinking back, I'm glad I kissed you the night of the dance." He gnnned again. "Consider all apologies withdrawn. I'll value that lucky moment all my life."

The warmth in her cheeks became scarlet. She looked away. "Thank you, kind sir. That gives me back my self-respect. Now, are you satisfied that this part of Hackamore's precious possessions is still intact?"

His manner sobered. "Don't you go cynical on me, young 'un."

He let his glance run once more over the gulf of country ahead and below, then swung his horse around. "We'll be getting back. What's here will keep, I reckon."

That was when the bullet struck.

The slug, striking just inches in front of Carlin's right leg, drove through the heavy leather of the saddle skirt and into his horse, and right after that came the distant, whipping report of a rifle. The horse, shaken by the impact, hunched for a split second, then gave a wild, stricken lunge. Carlin kicked free of the stirrups and as the horse went to its knees and then toppled over on its side, he swung clear, sliding a yard or so down slope before his gouging boot heels dug in and held him. His yell crackled at his companion.

"Get around the point — quick!"

Instead, she swung her horse between him and that distant threat. "No!" she cried. "Not without you, Leach!"

Carlin wasted no time arguing. He caught the rein of her horse and hauled it plunging after him to the safety he'd indicated. He heard the spiteful echoes of a second distant report, then another and another. But there was no further snap and whine of hurtling lead, and even in the confusion and black anger of the moment Carlin found time to wonder about this.

He came to a stop below the shelter of the point. "Get down!" he ordered harshly. "I want your horse."

She knew what he intended, so stayed in her saddle. "No! You're not riding up there. That was a rifle and you have only your

127

revolver. You wouldn't have a chance. No — Leach!"

He caught at her, pulled her from the saddle, tried to put her aside. But she wouldn't stay there. She swarmed back at him, caught hold of him, fought with all her slim strength.

"No!" she cried. "I won't let you. I won't let you go back up there and be shot. Leach — you idiot — no!" She was half sobbing. She wrapped her arms around him, hung on.

Abruptly he went still. "All right," he said. "All right, Dallas."

She had never seen him this way before. His face was harsh as graven rock, the blue of his eyes turning so dark it was like a smoky purple. She let out her relief in a little wail.

"You see, Leach — you see? It's what I meant — Dan Brandon's fight. And now it's you they're trying to kill!"

He looked down at her and seemed to come back from some great distance. The rigidity ran out of him. His tone smoothed, went gently gruff.

"I won't give them another chance. Stay here!"

He went back around the point, crouching, then crawling to the crest to make a long and careful survey of the country above and beyond. He could guess at the approximate angle from which the shot had come, and could place its source within reasonable limits. Out there now was no further sound or movement of any kind. The world lay bland and deceitfully still.

Then, off to the left and well up toward the head of a side gulch, a raven launched into flight. It was just a black dot at this distance, yet the flicker of movement caught Carlin's eye. He centered his gaze there just in time to see a horse and rider break from the gulch, cross a low saddle and dip from sight into the tangle beyond. The distance was too far for indentification of any kind, and that rider was spurring fast. Carlin turned and called down to Dallas.

"All clear. Bring your horse up. I'm going to get my saddle."

Carlin's horse lay on its off side, so he was able to loosen the latigo and free the cinch. He stripped off the headstall, ran the loop of Dallas Renfro's rope around the neck of the luckless beast. He gave Dallas a nod.

"Downhill."

She threw a dally around her saddle horn, set her buckskin pony to the pull, while from above Carlin gripped horn and cantle of his own rig and dug in his heels. The pull of the girl's rope slid the dead animal downhill a few feet and Carlin worked his saddle free.

He tossed off the girl's rope and as she drew it to her, coiling it, he carried his saddle and headstall down to her.

"You'll have to walk it a bit until we find a place to cache my gear."

She stepped from her saddle and watched silently while he loaded his saddle across her own, then strode along beside him as they moved off, leading the buckskin. Color was ebbing back into her face, but her eyes were grave and shadowed. She stole a glance at him. He sensed it and returned it.

"If I was a mite rough with you back there, I'm sorry, Dallas. Everything's all right now."

She shook her bead. "Everything isn't all right. That — that was terrible." She shivered a little. "Leach, you mustn't go on bossing Hackamore. It isn't fair to ask it of you. I — I'll tell Martha Brandon so."

"No," he said evenly, "no, you won't. You're not thinking straight just now. Later, you will." The bite of harshness roughened his tone again. "Somebody's asked for a fight. They're going to get one!"

They went back on foot as far as the Indian Mounds and there, under the overhang of an outcrop of rock, cached Carlin's saddle. Then, when Dallas stepped into her saddle again, Carlin swung up behind her. And they rode this way back to Sawbuck headquarters, letting the buckskin take its own time under the double load.

Bois Renfro had finished his job on the ranch-house roof, was now puttering around the corrals. He stared in silence as they rode up, then growled, "Something happened. What?"

"Somebody took a shot," Carlin explained briefly. "Missed me, but killed my horse. I'll be borrowing a bronc and a saddle from you for a couple of days, Bois."

"Sure. Help yourself." Renfro's eyes pinched down as he toted up the significance of this thing. "How far was Dallas from you at the time of the shot?"

Carlin indicated a corral post some ten feet away. "About so."

"The damned whelp!" Renfro exploded. "He might have hit her."

Carlin nodded. "Something I'm going to remember — and add to the reckoning."

"Any idea who?"

"Not the slightest. But I expect to raise a lot of dust to find out."

"Where did it happen?"

Carlin told him and Renfro pondered this grimly for a moment. "What's so damned valuable about that range, anyhow? You

131

think Case Broderick was behind that try at you, Leach?"

Carlin shrugged. "You guess."

Bois Renfro looked at his daughter, a silent listener to it all. He marked the shadow in her eyes and tried to lighten it with a bit of ponderous humor.

"You better pick another riding partner, youngster. This fellow Carlin shapes up as dangerous company."

"That's not a bit funny, Dad," she retorted. "I don't think it will do a bit of good, but you might try and persuade Leach that he doesn't really owe a thing to Hackamore. Why should he be asked to carry on old quarrels that Dan Brandon started?"

"Wouldn't put it quite that way," rumbled Renfro soberly. "A lot of quarrels were pointed at Dan that he never started and didn't want. Other men, jealous of him, did the starting. Besides, Leach is a man grown. He knows his own mind."

Carlin went into the cavvy corral, caught up one of Renfro's saddle broncs. Renfro brought a saddle from a shed, stood silent as Carlin cinched it into place. Then he murmured, "It was luck for you in a way, Leach. You'll know what to look for, and to keep off ridge tops."

"Ridge tops — and other places," Carlin

132

remarked dryly. "I'll see that you have this horse and gear before too long."

"Any time, man — any time."

Dallas had gone over to the ranch house and stood now in the doorway. Carlin pulled up there, looking down at her gravely.

"Lot of champion in you, Dallas. Thanks for going along. And in case I'm lucky enough to warrant it, don't worry too much about me and Hackamore."

"Darn Hackamore!" she said emphatically. "I believe in people managing their own lives, not letting some ranch do it for them."

"Not always that easy," said Carlin. "One ties in with the other. Now, how's for a smile before I leave?"

She showed him one and followed it with a little sigh. "I just can't stay mad at you, it seems. And I won't worry about you. No man is worth it — they're such contrary critters."

Carlin grinned. "That's better. When you get sassy, then I know you're back to normal."

He rode away and she stood for a little time, looking after him. She rubbed her right hand over her upper left arm. Back there, when he'd pulled her off her horse, he'd been rougher than he thought. But she

133

didn't mind. It was the kind of hurt that put a soft glow in her eyes. She went on into the house.

Carlin held to a steady jog, all the way back to Hackamore. He did a lot of thinking as he rode, his face pulled into grim lines and a glimmer of that dark anger building again, far back in his eyes. About the real identity of the gulcher, he could only guess. But the fact that the fellow had been laying out, waiting, there below the Indian Mound, was significant. Case Broderick, knowing that his ultimatum about the range was virtually certain to draw Carlin down there for a look-see, could have arranged the whole thing. For it was a perfect place for that kind of a murder. A man could lie dead and unfound in one of those tangled, brush-choked draws until his bones turned to mold.

But again, this might be an entirely erroneous line of reasoning. That distant, isolated range, with rarely a rider through it, yet with some cattle there, would be a perfect place for some solitary rustler or slow-elker to work, picking up a few head now and then and selling the meat to the grangers on the plains below the river gap. Could be, thought Carlin, that he and Dallas had shown on the scene at a time when such petty thievery was going on and the renegade, spooked at the chance of discovery, had either lost his head, or deliberately made sure that he wouldn't be trailed. Maybe he hadn't tried for Carlin at all, but just dropped Carlin's horse to put him afoot. Maybe — !

Carlin swung his shoulders restlessly. A man could cook up a thousand damned maybes. A twinge in his wounded arm brought him solidly back to that definite reality. No maybes there — no maybes at all!

Of only one thing, he mused bleakly, could he be sure. Somebody wanted him out of the picture — and bad! Two attempts on his life in the space of a few hours. There was no mistaking the cardinal fact that both he and Hackamore had their enemies and that, for better or worse, he was Hackamore.

Far back in the country beyond the Indian Mounds, Hitch Wheeler was squatted on a high point, rifle across his knees, a cigarette coiling smoke up past his narrow, sardonic face. From that point of vantage he'd watched Leach Carlin and Dallas Renfro free Carlin's saddle from his stricken horse, watched them trudge away leading Dallas' mount, with Carlin's gear loaded on it. And after they had vanished completely from sight, he stayed just as he was for another couple of hours, stoic as an Indian. Again and again his glance swept the country below him.

At long last he straightened to his feet, laying a final glance on the sprawled blot of color that was Leach Carlin's dead horse, then swinging his survey to another ridge point closer to him, between himself and the spot where the horse lay. He shrugged, grinned in his reckless, unreadable way, then prowled back from the point where his own horse stood tied and hidden in a brush clump. He mounted and rode off, cutting a guarded, circular course across the big sweep of country.

CHAPTER SIX

Joe Spence watched Leach Carlin dismount, then walked around horse and rider in a small circle.

"That's not the bronc you rode out on and that's not your kak. What happened?"

While unsaddling, Carlin told him. Joe swore harshly. "The hell! You see anybody?"

"Just a glimpse while he was ducking out, but too far away to tell a thing."

"Maybe an idea of Broderick's, Leach?"

"Maybe. And then again, it could have been sheer accident. Somebody might have been after a deer — there's some big ones in that country. There were those other shots that came after the first one, but with no lead flying my way."

Joe grunted skeptically. "With the guy pulling out in a hurry the way he did?"

"Why not?" shrugged Carlin. "He could have spooked after he realized what he'd done. Again, he could have been some two-bit rustler or slow-elker, not wanting company."

Joe shook his head. "Can't go along with you there. That feller was hid to begin with. And after putting you afoot, all he had to do was stay hid. Come right down to it, he didn't need to have throwed a slug your way at all if he didn't want to be seen. All he had to do was lay low until you'd gone your way. No, sir — I don't go for this accident idea, or the rustler one, either. First's too far-fetched and the other don't add up right. That hombre was trying for your hide, Leach. Why he should have spooked after-wards — well, to begin with, a gulcher is a damn coward or he wouldn't be a gulcher. Was I you, I'd hunt up Mister Case Broderick and ask him some damn straight questions."

"What good would that do?" said Carlin. "He'd probably lie. Sure to, in fact."

"Mebbe so," admitted Joe. "But I'd ask 'em anyhow."

Carlin turned his horse into the corral. "Clint get home all right?"

"Expect so, though I ain't seen him. That silver-mounted kak of his is in the shed. He's probably nursing a head; from what Sam Desmond said he sure was wallowing deep in the liquor pot. You want I should scout that Indian Mound range and bring in your saddle?"

138

"Not alone, Joe. Tomorrow you and Jimmy Spurlock can drift down that way. Take Bois Renfro's horse and gear back to him. But ride easy and watch yourselves. Don't get sucked into any row you can't handle."

Carlin went over to the office and let himself in. He took the desk chair and slouched down in it, building up a smoke. His wounded arm was bothering him a little and he clamped his right hand around it, his thoughts running dark and frustrated.

A step sounded beyond the inner door and Martha Brandon came in. Carlin started to get to his feet, but she nodded him back into his chair, while pulling up another for herself.

"Clint made a dismal fool of himself in town, didn't he?" she asked quietly. "He came in just at dawn this morning and went to bed. His room smells like a distillery."

There was a low note of bitterness in her voice that made Carlin stir uncomfortably.

"He's not the first to try and drown his troubles in a whiskey bottle, Mrs. Brandon."

"A poor refuge," she said curtly. She looked at him keenly. "That was one of Bois Renfro's horses you rode in on, Leach. I've seen him on it more than once. What happened to your own?" Then when he hesitated, she added, "The truth, Leach. There must be no evasion between us, no evasion of any kind."

So he told her, while she listened in grave reflection. She put her elbow on the arm of her chair, cupped her chin in her hand, while she stared into her thoughts. Then she straightened and met his glance.

"I feel very guilty, Leach. I see now that I had no right to ask you to assume a burden you had no hand in building. I knew there were men who hated Dan, and who asked nothing better than a chance to tear down what he had built. But I did not think them ruthless enough to dare outright, cowardly murder. I've no right to ask you to gamble your life for me and the memory of my dead husband. I'm giving you back your promise, Leach."

"Which of course I won't agree to," he said. "I went into this deal with my eyes open. I knew it wouldn't be a soft ride and I'm not asking for one. There was sure to be rough work. Just because it's shown itself this early in the game is no reason why I should shy off, or that you should, either. Don't you feel guilty about anything."

She watched him, her eyes softening. "That good strong shoulder," she murmured. "You were doing some heavy thinking when I came in. Any answers, so far?"

He shook his head. "There's one I wish I had. Maybe you can help me there. That Steptoe Creek–Indian Mounds range. Why did Dan Brandon take it up, why did he keep it? Frankly, Mrs. Brandon, as cattle range it isn't worth bothering with."

"I've never seen the range," she admitted. "I remember when Dan first ordered a small herd of cattle thrown on it, saying at the time that you had to put cattle on a range if you wanted to hold it. In my younger years I might have ridden down for a look at it, more from curiosity than anything else. As it was, I really never gave it much thought, beyond the fact that Dan had taken it over."

"And he never talked about it to you?"

"Not to any extent. I wasn't particularly curious. To me it was just another deal Dan had closed and I figured he had his good reasons for doing so. I do recall him saying something about picking up the range for a fair price."

Carlin straightened in his chair. "Then he did — buy it?"

"Oh, yes. From a man with some sort of Spanish name. I can't recall it now."

Carlin exclaimed with satisfaction. "Then Hackamore's claim to it is really solid! That

141

helps. And if Dan Brandon laid out hard money for it, he saw real value in it some- where. Mrs. Brandon, I think we should go through all of his papers and records care- fully. Maybe the answer we're looking for is there somewhere. Is that all right with you?"

"Of course, Leach. And I'll help you. Dan was a great one for keeping records. He used to say that if a man didn't know where he stood five years ago, then how could he know whether he was going ahead or behind to- day?"

There was a closet in one corner of the office. Its shelves were stacked with papers and ranch records of all kinds, some of which ran back as far as fifteen years. There were tally records, expense sheets, items of upkeep and repair. There were payrolls and banking records and business transactions of a dozen different kinds. And there were numbers of penciled memorandums, jotted down here and there in a bold, angular hand.

"He left nothing to memory, did he?" re- marked Carlin.

"Nothing," was Martha Brandon's gravely wistful reply. "Nothing except the great things in his life. And these he stored away within himself and never forgot. Like my birthdays, for instance, and the anniversary of our marriage. He never overlooked things of that sort. Often it wasn't much that he brought to me, perhaps just a handful of wild flowers, or a sprig off some colorful wild shrub. But it was always something —."

The afternoon ran out while they worked, sorting over every item they could find. At twilight Carlin lit a lamp and Martha Brandon went out to prepare a bite of supper. Carlin went on at his chore, and tucked back in a corner on one of the closet shelves he found a small, stout wooden box, packed with papers and items of a more personal nature than the rest of the ranch records. The top item in it was an envelope, unsealed. Carlin's expression sobered as he looked over the contents.

There were several pages torn from a small pocket notebook. Each page was an I.O.U., signed by Sam Desmond. Making a swift mental addition of the amounts listed, Carlin came up with a total just short of six thousand dollars.

He spun up another smoke, musing. Here, he thought, was one big reason for Sam Desmond having played the tail to Brandon's kite. Carlin replaced the contents in the envelope and went on with his search. And a little deeper in the box he found what he was looking for.

It was a bill of sale, written in a fine hand, describing the physical limits of a parcel of range which Carlin had no difficulty in identifying as that which lay between the Indian Mounds and Steptoe Creek. For the sum of twenty-five hundred dollars it transferred the title of this land from one Manuel Quesada to Dan Brandon, and was signed by this Manuel Quesada. At the bottom of the paper Brandon had added a penciled memorandum of his own. It ran:

This deal is a gamble I may or may not live to see come out one way or another. But there is a lot of granger country on the plains below the river gap and the day could come when use will be found for all the water now running to waste in the river. It will be worth $2500 to find out what kind of guesser I am.

Carlin was reading the rough document over a seeond time when Martha Brandon returned, carrying a tray of sandwiches and a pot of coffee. She saw the triumph in Carlin's eye.

"You've found something, Leach?"

He tapped the paper with his finger. "Right

here. The answer we were looking for. Read it."

She put the tray on the desk, read, then showed a puzzled frown. "I'm not sure I understand what Dan meant by a gamble."

"That river water," explained Carlin. "How could men put it to use on the lower plains? Just one way. For irrigation. And that would mean a dam. Where would such a dam be built? At the only logical spot; in the canyon narrows, just this side of where Steptoe Creek cuts into the canyon from the west. So, for twenty-five hundred dollars, Dan bought not only the site of such a dam, but most of the country the lake behind such a dam would cover. Should that dam ever be built, the land would be worth a lot of money, many, many times what he paid for it. That's the gamble he meant."

"But I've never heard a word, much less seen any evidence of such a dam being even considered, Leach."

"Neither have I," he admitted. "But that doesn't mean someone else couldn't have picked up the word, through some channel of their own."

"You mean Case Broderick?"

"Perhaps. Certainly if the idea occurred to Dan Brandon, it could occur to someone else. And offer the one legitimate reason why they'd be anxious to get hold of the piece of range."

Martha Brandon pulled up her chair, poured coffee.

"And they're willing to have a man shot in the back to clear the way."

"Men have done as much, or worse, for less," Carlin said.

"And having failed once, may try again," murmured Martha Brandon. "Leach, I'm afraid. Not for myself, but for you. Money, possession, isn't everything. We've the main fabric of Hackamore to work with. Let Broderick have that range. We've Dan's opinion that it could be only a gamble anyhow, and probably it will always be just that."

Carlin shook a stubborn head. "Maybe not a gamble. Broderick must know something. As for letting it go, that's out of the question. You don't buy peace by being weak, Mrs. Brandon. In a showdown like this we can't be half one thing, half something else. We fight for all of Hackamore, or for none of it. In this Quesada deed it seems we have honest title to the river gap range. So — we keep it!"

Martha Brandon sighed. "Very well, Leach. You're right, of course. I won't question the matter again. You're going to inquire about the possibility of such a dam?"

"Tomorrow morning. I'll talk it over with Lyle Barnard. It's possible that through banking circles he may find out something."

They finished their evening snack and then Carlin spoke with a slow reluctance. "I've found something else in this box, Mrs. Brandon. Maybe you know of it, maybe you don't. But if you don't, you should."

She looked at him in that keen way of hers. "What is it, Leach?"

"Several I.O.U.s. Signed by Sam Desmond, and totaling right on six thousand dollars. Representing, of course, money your husband loaned Desmond at one time or another."

"I knew nothing of that. Let me see them."

Carlin built a smoke and sat in silence while she looked over the contents of the envelope. She shook her white head slowly.

"Poor Sam! He'll never in the world be able to pay these. We may as well destroy them."

"No!" said Carlin swiftly. "You never know about such things. Dan saved them. So will we."

She was thoughtful for a moment before nodding. "Very well. We'll save them. But they'll stay in this box and we'll never mention them unless Sam Desmond brings up the subject. And we'll never press him for the money. He was one of Dan's oldest friends."

In his room, Clint had slept off his drunk. He had a savage head on him, but was surlily sober, and craved water in large quantities. He was thinking of heading for the kitchen when his mother passed along the hall just outside his bedroom door. He heard her turn into the office and close the door there. Then, as he stepped into the hall himself, Clint heard the murmur of voices in the office. He moved quietly to the office door and listened, a spasm of anger twisting his face as he heard Leach Carlin speaking.

But as the import of Carlin's words struck home, Clint listened more intently. He heard what Carlin had to say and what Martha Brandon had to say. Clint forgot his aching head and a sharpening light began to burn in his bleared eyes. And when he heard sounds indicating the conference in the office was about to break up, he slipped back into his room and closed the door. He sat on the edge of his bed in the darkness, mulling over what he'd heard and as the portent and possibilities of it all came to him more clearly, he smiled to himself, slyly triumphant. He set himself to wait until the night was far advanced and the ranch fully asleep.

Lyle Barnard, leisurely savoring an after-breakfast cigar, stood on the hotel porch and watched Leach Carlin come jogging along the street. Carlin pulled in at the hitch rail and swung down. Barnard saluted him with his cigar.

"You ride early this morning, Leach. A reason?"

Carlin nodded. "Little talk with you."

The banker pulled a bucket chair out to the edge of the porch where the slanting morning sunlight struck. "Listening," he said briefly.

Carlin settled on the edge of the porch, spun up a cigarette. "Ever hear any talk about a dam being built along the river, Lyle?"

Barnard swung an alert head. "A dam — on Big Sage River? Where — and by whom?"

"At the narrows in the river-gap canyon. By whom, I wouldn't know."

Barnard took a long pull at his cigar, then murmured, "Interesting possibility. But you're the first I ever heard mention it. Considerable undertaking, and for what purpose?"

"Lot of granger country below the gap. Country that could use irrigation water."

"Something there, all right," admitted Barnard. "But you didn't pick this idea out of thin air. Where'd you get it?"

"By adding up this and that." Carlin went on to tell of the ultimatum that had been given Martha Brandon the day of Dan's funeral. "As cattle range," he added, "the stretch really isn't worth bothering with. But Dan owned it and Case Broderick seems to want it — bad. So, I got to wondering. Yesterday evening Mrs. Brandon and I went through a lot of Dan's old records. We found that Dan Brandon bought the stretch from one Manuel Quesada. Paid twenty-five hundred for it. On the deed, Dan added a few remarks as a sort of note. Said he'd bought on a gamble, because he felt that maybe some day all the water now running to waste in the river might be used on those lower plains by the grangers. He didn't actually mention a dam, but he sure suggested the possibility. So, what do you think?"

The banker squinted thoughtfully. "I've never been down that way, so I don't know the lay of the country at all. In your opinion, Leach, would a dam be practical there?"

"Perfect place. Back up a big lake of water, too."

"And the limits of this piece of range would take in the site of the dam, as well as the country the lake would cover?"

"That's right."

Barnard took his cigar from his lips, flicked the ash off carefully, smiled with a faint musing. "Mighty shrewd old codger, Dan was. Didn't miss any tricks. Now a project of that kind would be too much for the kind of private capital we have around here. It would have to be pretty much a government job. And should that take place, then that piece of range would be worth many times the twenty-five hundred dollars Brandon paid for it. Yes, sir — he was a shrewd old fox."

Carlin stirred. "Reason I'm unloading to you, Lyle, is the thought that maybe through banking circles you could find out if the government is considering such a project. On the quiet, I mean, so as not to advertise our hand."

"Could be," murmured Barnard. "I've some connections who, in the course of business, keep pretty close tabs on appropriation bills. I'll get off a couple of letters concerning the matter." The banker waved his cigar, with a little show of excitement. "You know, Leach, I've a feeling that you've struck a hot trail, one that opens up a lot of thinking and supplies some answers to things I've casually wondered about."

Carlin's head came up. "Like what?"

"Men, for one thing," chuckled Barnard softly. "I believe I remarked the other evening that Mister Mike Quarney was a self-contained sort, much alone. But not entirely. On occasion I've seen him pass more than the time of day with Case Broderick. Do you grasp the inference?"

"Some. Go on."

"Ex-Senator Mike Quarney. Once a well-known figure around Washington, and bound to have made many contacts there. No doubt he still has some, which could mean channels through which he could get advance information on many things. Like water-power projects, and such, which the government might be contemplating. Friend Leach, I think you'd be smart if, when you look at Case Broderick and his announced intentions, you see if you can't discern the shadow of Mike Quarney at Broderick's shoulder."

Carlin's eyes pinched down in thought. He let out a deep, slow breath. "If Dan Brandon was a smart fox, you're two of them, Lyle. You go write those letters." He stood up. "And no use starting any rumors, Lyle."

The banker smiled. "I grow closer-mouthed every day. I'll let you know what answers I get, as soon as I get them."

Moving back down street, Carlin saw Ace Lanier in the doorway of the Skyhigh. Ace had been sweeping out and now stood leaning on his broom, surveying the new day. He lifted a hand.

"The souse get home all right?"

Carlin nodded. "Still nursing a sore head, I suspect."

Ace shook his head in disgust. "That Clint! I've watched him grow up. Smooth, slick, sly. In my book, no damn good! How a man like Dan ever sired such, beats me. No finer people ever lived than Dan and Martha Brandon. Kind of takes apart this theory on blood lines, doesn't it?"

Carlin's expression showed absolutely nothing. "Throwbacks come along in humans as well as animals, Ace."

"I guess so. Sam Desmond get hold of you?"

"No. He was looking for me?"

"Night before last. Came in a little while after that stud game broke up. I was about ready to close for the night. He asked for you. I told him you said you were going to stay the night in town and if he'd get right over to the hotel he'd probably catch you awake. He said as long as you'd turned in,

153

he wouldn't bother you, but see you some other time. He had something on his mind. Seemed worried, or something. He had a couple of drinks, then left. Looked like he might have been hitting a bottle on the side. You know, Leach, there's another feller I can't figure. Seems to have softened up and run to ragged edges in the past couple of years."

Carlin, remembering the I.O.U.s he'd found among Brandon's records, said, "Think I know what's bothering Sam. I'll see him. And Ace, as a favor to Mrs. Brandon, if not to me, should Clint show up again, wanting to swim in the stuff, sort of do what you can to tone him down, will you?"

"All right," conceded the saloon owner gruffly. "Three drinks will be his limit, and if he tries to argue with me I'll wipe up the floor with him. Damn people who are a nuisance to everybody else!" Ace made another vigorous swipe with his broom and would have turned back into his saloon, had not Carlin, struck with another thought, halted him with a question.

"You're one of the old-timers on the prairie, Ace. Ever hear of a fellow named Manuel Quesada?"

Ace rubbed a reflective finger alongside his

broken nose. "Quesada — Quesada?" he mumbled. Then, brightening — "Oh, sure — I remember him! Used to have a cabin somewhere down the river. He'd come into town once in a while for grub and generally stop in here for a drink or two. Haven't seen him in so long, I'd plumb forgotten him. What about him?"

Carlin shrugged enigmatically. "Just wondering. Happened to hear the name mentioned. Anyhow, thanks."

As Carlin stirred his horse to movement again, a rider turned in at the far end of the street and came along at a shuffling jog, pulling in at the rail in front of Billy Prior's store. Carlin recognized the lank, easily slouched figure of Hitch Wheeler, who did not dismount immediately, but instead stayed in his saddle, watching Carlin approach. He showed a faint smile and a slight tip of his head.

"Glad to see you in good health this fine morning, Carlin."

It was the inflection of tone rather than the actual portent of the man's words that made Carlin rein in and meet his glance.

Along with others, Carlin had done his share of wondering about this fellow. Hitch Wheeler, this footloose, restless fellow who never had a steady job; who came and went without apparent purpose or concern; who held his own counsel and laid a warding wall between himself and other men. Carlin had heard all manner of conjecture about the man and the charges that he lived mainly off the beef of other men. Brandon had held to this theory, Carlin knew. But also, as far as Carlin was aware, no one had ever been able to back up conjecture with real proof.

Privately, Carlin had never held anything against Wheeler. If Hitch Wheeler liked to live his aimless, lone-wolf existence, that, as Carlin saw it, was Wheeler's own business. And until somebody produced something better than mere talk as proof, Carlin wasn't going to blame the man for anything. Just now, Carlin was remembering how Wheeler had made certain people take off their hats the day of Dan Brandon's funeral, so he matched Wheeler's faint smile and answered easily.

"Hello, Hitch. My health's about as usual. Anything lead you to expect it might be otherwise?"

Wheeler shrugged. "You're a big man on the prairie, now. And maybe blocking the trail of certain people. The health of a man in that spot is always a chancy thing. And I say again I'm glad to see yours is good."

Carlin spun up a cigarette, then handed

across the makings, always a gesture of good will. "Ever consider staying in one spot long enough to hold down a steady job, Hitch?"

Wheeler built his smoke slowly and with care. Not until he had finished and lipped the cigarette did his head lift. His twisted, sardonic grin was working again.

"Now who would offer me a steady job? I'm Hitch Wheeler, a bad one. Didn't you know that, Carlin? I live off the other fellow's beef — and even scare little children, so some people claim. I'm no good. I'm just a coyote who walks on two legs instead of four. You just ask most anybody and they'll tell you that."

His tone was light, his words mocking. Yet it seemed to Carlin that for just a short moment he'd seen past the front of that mocking indifference and glimpsed a shade of loneliness and bitterness.

"There's a steady job for you at Hackamore," Carlin said quietly, "if you'd care to sign on. As for the rest, I never did go for empty talk. Be a lot of satisfacion in making the loose talkers eat their words."

Hitch Wheeler sucked deep on his cigarette, stared straight ahead, his face sober. "You mean that?" he asked slowly. "You'd really give me a riding job at Hackamore?"

"That's right, Hitch. And happy to."

Wheeler dismounted, tied his horse, then came swiftly around. "Why?"

"Because Hackamore could use another good hand."

Wheeler leaned against the rail, looking at the ground, a restless boot scuffing the dust. "I'll think on it," he said slowly. "Yeah, I'll think on it."

He ducked under the rail and went into the store.

Carlin headed on out for the ranch and some two miles from town, met up with Clint Brandon, heading in. Clint was looking fairly normal again, having shaved and cleaned up. He gave Carlin a hard stare and would have gone on by with that. But Carlin swung his horse across the trail.

"Just a minute, Clint. Gotta couple of things to say to you."

"Not a damn bit interested in anything you have to say," was Clint's surly retort. He would have reined his horse wide and passed on, but hauled up short as Carlin's voice hit at him with an abrupt, savage harshness.

"You'll listen, if I have to drag you out of that saddle by the scruff of the neck!"

The tone, the words, jolted Clint. He stared his settled, solid hatred. But he couldn't stand up to Carlin's cold survey. He stirred in his saddle, looked away.

"All right. Have your say and get it over with."

Carlin sagged his weight in his off stirrup, rested his crossed forearms on his saddle horn. "It seems," he said slowly, "that I've inherited a pretty rough job. Maybe a little rougher than I first figured, considering the things that have happened in the past few days. So it behooves me to take the gloves off, starting now! If you'd work with me, it would help a lot. But I know you never will, so we'll waste no more time over that angle. However, I'm telling you for the last time that I'm going to have no more patience with you."

"Am I asking you to?" retorted Clint. "Am I asking a damn thing of you except that you leave me alone and mind your own business?"

Carlin went on as though he hadn't heard. "I've a great deal of admiration and respect for Martha Brandon. She's been a good mother to you, far better than you deserve. Not too long ago she buried her husband, a man who broke his heart trying to make a man out of you. She's been hurt enough. So get this! You get soused again, you'll know the roughest sobering up anybody ever went through. I'll see to that — personally!"

Clint sneered. "Any time I need a keeper, I'll let you know."

Carlin straightened in his saddle, and his voice was whiplash sharp. "And finally, don't ever try and cut me with a knife again!"

The sneer on Clint's face turned to an expression of open bewilderment. He blinked.

"Cut you with a knife! Just what the hell kind of crazy talk is that?"

Carlin measured him with narrow-eyed judgment and had to admit that here for once was no guile. Clint plainly had no idea what he'd meant by reference to a knife. Carlin touched his horse with the spur and gave out his final word as he swung by.

"All right — forget it. It didn't happen. But for the rest, you'd better believe what I've told you."

Heading along for town, Clint gave vent to a short flurry of cursing, but without any great amount of venom. For he was packing a secret all his own, and his eyes glinted with the triumph of it.

On reaching town, Clint wandered about for a time, apparently with no purpose in mind at all. But all the time his eyes were busy searching up and down street. He observed with satisfaction that it was virtually deserted. A single saddle bronc besides his own was all that was in sight. It stood at the rail in front of Billy Prior's store, hipshot, switching languidly at flies.

Clint turned in at the Skyhigh. Ace Lanier looked at him with no friendliness at all.

"Don't ask for a bottle. You can't have it."

"Keep your damned bottle," retorted Clint. "All I want is one drink."

Ace poured him one. "You've had it."

Clint flipped a coin on the bar, gulped the drink, and went out. Over the space of time it took to twist up a cigarette, he made another survey of the street. Then he turned and sauntered a little way south, cut quickly into an alley and hurried along.

Over on the porch of Billy Prior's store, Hitch Wheeler moved into view, carrying a flour sack containing a few items of groceries. He tied this behind the cantle of his saddle, then drifted at a long angle across the street at an easy, idle stride until he came to the mouth of the same alley Clint had ducked into. He turned in here and immediately his casual manner disappeared. He straightened and moved faster.

Breaking out of the alley at the rear, he was just in time to see Clint cutting along toward a house set well back from the southern end of the street. Mike Quarney's house. Wheeler used the corner of the building at his left as a post of concealment, and from here kept his narrowed, unreadable watch of Clint. He saw Clint close in on Quarney's house with a certain furtiveness, finally hurrying up the steps and knocking.

Mike Quarney opened the door. There was a short exchange of words, with Clint emphasizing his remarks with an impatient gesture. Then he and Quarney went into the house and the door closed.

Hitch Wheeler stayed just as he was while he built and smoked a cigarette, his head bent in thought. Then he turned and came back up the alley to Bidwell Street again.

CHAPTER SEVEN

At Hackamore headquarters there was a buckboard pulled up by the corrals and Carlin rode in. He was just in time to see Martha Brandon greeting two other women at the front door of the ranch house, Dallas Renfro and her mother. Dallas turned at the sound of Carlin's horse, lifted an arm in a quick wave before she disappeared.

Carlin put up his horse and then went over to the office and settled himself behind the desk, held in the grip of dark and frustrating thought. He was still at it some half hour later and coming up with no good answers, when the inner door opened and Dallas came in. She pulled up a chair, settled into it, folded her hands in her lap and looked at him, smiling.

"By his scowl," she observed, "the man is in a temper. I hope he doesn't roar and swear at me."

Carlin leaned back, and the hard-pulled lines of his face softened. "Only one thing could make me roar and swear at you. That would be if you said anything to Mrs. Bran-

163

don about it not being fair to ask me to shoulder any of Dan's quarrels. You more or less threatened to, you know."

She sighed. "Yes, I know. Maybe I still feel that way about it. But I won't say anything to her."

"That," approved Carlin, "is being a good little girl. And earns you a pat on your pretty head for obedience."

That pretty head tossed slightly. "Not obedience — just discretion. And no desire to worry or hurt her further. She was so awful glad to see mother. I think mother is good for her, Leach."

"Bound to be," he nodded. "And you're good for me. There's something about you. Just seeing you picks a man up."

Color stole through her cheeks. "Look out that the man doesn't drop with a dull thud, my friend."

Carlin showed a faint smile. "Once you had me fooled. No more. That cloak of stickeriness you put on is all a bluff. Underneath it, you're a pretty swell person."

Her dress was starched gingham, simplicity itself. She wore it with a cool, clean grace. Her color deepened under Carlin's frankly approving regard.

"Let's get away from the subject of me. Joe Spence and Jimmy Spurlock were by this morning, bringing back Dad's horse and gear. Said they were on their way to the Indian Mounds to get your saddle. Both of them had rifles slung under their stirrups. It set me to thinking and I got scared all over again. The sight of those rifles made Dad pretty thoughtful, too."

"Getting to be that kind of a range, it seems," added Carlin gravely. "But don't you get in a stew about it. Everything will be all right."

"You say that easily enough, Leach. But I'm an awful coward."

"A coward, she says," murmured Carlin. "Hm-m! Let's see. As I remember it, my horse had just gone down. I yelled to the lady, telling her to get around the point and out of sight. Did she go? Not much! Instead, she swung her horse and herself between me and where the shot had come from. She wouldn't get out of there until I did. Some coward!"

"I was scared silly," declared Dallas hurriedly. "I didn't know what I was doing. If I hadn't been too scared to think, I'd have run for dear life. I would — really."

Carlin's smile was teasing. "Charming little liar," drawled.

Dallas got to her feet. "Just like a man — always ready to believe the worst of a woman.

165

Sir, I leave you to your scowls and growls."

She started to, but happened to glance through a window as she turned. What she saw stopped her. Out there by the corrals another buckboard had just pulled in. Driving it was Beth Desmond. Dallas turned back.

"Of course," she said tartly, "if you'll apologise, I'll stay a little longer."

Out there by the corrals, Beth Desmond stared fixedly at the other buckboard and saw, burned into the back of the seat, Bois Renfro's Sawbuck brand. She hesitated a moment, her glance swinging to the ranch house. In sudden decision she got down, tied her team, then came straight over to the office, knocking at the outer door. At Carlin's summons she came in, moving with a little swagger.

"If I'm intruding — ?" She left the question hanging.

You are and you know it, thought Dallas privately. Aloud, and very sweetly, she said, "Of course not. Leach and I were spatting, as usual. Now he won't dare call me names."

Carlin blinked, a little bewildered. Which went to prove that he knew little of the nuances of feminine nature. Beth perched on a corner of the desk, a move contrived to sug-

166

gest a certain intimacy between herself and Carlin. She swung a booted foot nonchalantly and put the full warmth of her smile on Carlin.

"Poor man! Along with his other troubles he has women to fight."

Dallas gritted her teeth, sensing defeat coming up. The next moment she could have boxed Carlin's ears, and hugged him at the same time.

"Oh, no, Beth," he said. "Dallas and me argue, but we never fight. She's the best little partner I know."

Just the faintest suggestion of a frown touched Beth's dark beauty. Silence fell, and a small demon of tautness lifted its head. Rescue came in the shape of Joe Spence and Jimmy Spurlock swinging in by the corrals on sweating, hard-ridden mounts. Joe stepped down and came bow-legging it hurriedly over to the office.

Carlin, hearing the rattle of hoofs, got to his feet and glanced out the window. He had the door opened as Joe arrived. Joe said flatly, "They've moved in below the Indian Mounds, Leach."

"Circle 60?" prompted Carlin.

Joe nodded. "Broderick's cows. Hadn't been there long. A lot of them were still bunched."

"See any riders?"

"Some. Randall and Shep Bowen. Frank Labine and Ward Dancy. Couple more that were strangers to me."

"Labine and Dancy, eh?" murmured Carlin. "Couple of quick-change lads, there. Well, it doesn't surprise me. They offered you and Jimmy no trouble, Joe?"

"It was there if we wanted it. Randall in particular as walking some stiff-legged and with his roach up. But I minded what you told me, so the kid and me, he let him paw and snort and then pulled out when he ordered us off. Kinda went against the grain. That jigger will figure now that I'm afraid of him. Next good chance I get I'm goin' to disabuse him on that score."

Carlin's glance was fixed on a far nothingness, the line of his jaw hardening. "They've thrown it right in our faces, Joe," he said finally.

"Yeah," nodded Joe. "Now what do we do?"

"Call them!" rapped Carlin harshly. "Go catch me up a bronc and a fresh one for yourself. Be right with you."

The inner office door opened and Martha Brandon came into the room. She hadn't missed the sound of Joe's and Jimmy Spurlock's hurried arrival.

"What is it, Leach?" she asked.

He turned to her. "Circle 60 cattle on the Indian Mounds range, Mrs. Brandon. Looks like Broderick's made good on his threat. I'm going to see him about it."

She came over to him, a stately, white-haired figure. She laid a hand on his arm and at what Carlin saw in her eyes he shook his head swiftly. "No change in our agreement, remember."

Her fingers tightened on his arm, then fell away. "Very well, Leach."

When he had first come into the office, Carlin had taken off his gunbelt and hung it on the back of the desk chair. Now he strapped on the weapon with quick hands. A change had come over him. His eyes had darkened and the ruggedness of his features seemed all bleak angles. Dallas Renfro watched him, her eyes very big, her face sober and paling slightly. He caught her glance and paused in front of her. His voice was curt, yet held a thread of gentleness.

"Now, now — nothing's ever as bad as it seems. One of these days we'll have time to finish our argument."

Joe Spence had returned to the corrals and was catching up the fresh horses. Jimmy Spurlock was freeing Carlin's saddle, which he'd brought in tied behind his own. He looked over at Joe.

"We going somewhere?"

"Leach and me," answered Joe. "Call on Mister Broderick, I reckon."

Five minutes later, Carlin and Joe were on their way.

From the door and window of the office, the three women watched them go. At least two of them, Martha and Dallas, knew that the short period of tense peace on Big Sage Prairie was definitely over. Now the gloves were off. What the future portended no one could say, except that it was sure to be wild and dark. Martha Brandon put an arm about Dallas' slender shoulders, an unconscious gesture, yet one into which Beth, standing at the window, read a special significance.

She looked at these two, standing there in the doorway, the elderly, white-haired woman, and the slim, shining-haired younger one, and a little spasm of anger pulled at her lips, while her dark eyes took on a sultriness. She was remembering who it was that Leach Carlin had spoken to as he was leaving. To Dallas Renfro, and with a certain gentleness, even in the deepening harshness of his mood. But for herself, not even a nod. She moved over to the door, pulling on her gauntlet gloves with quick, hard jerks.

Martha looked at her. "Beth, you're not leaving? We've had no time at all to visit. Nora Renfro's inside and now the four of us —."

Beth's head gesture of negation was almost curt. "Thanks. But I really must be getting along. I hadn't intended to stay. I just dropped by to say hello."

They let her by and watched her while she crossed to her buckboard, untied the team, stepped into the rig, and rolled away.

"She's stunning, isn't she, Mrs. Brandon?" murmured Dallas. "She's always so well dressed — and everything."

For a little time Martha Brandon did not answer. She was thinking of six thousand dollars of I.O.U.s signed by Sam Desmond. Finally she answered slowly, "I think that there goes the most selfish woman I've ever known."

Less than half an hour after Carlin and Joe Spence had spurred away, Jimmy Spurlock heard hoofs coming in. He stepped to the door of the bunkhouse, where he stopped stock-still to stare, as he recognized the new arrival. It was Hitch Wheeler. Jimmy walked slowly out to meet him.

"Something I can do for you, Hitch?"

The lank rider nodded gravely. "Carlin. Like a little talk with him."

"He's not here," said Jimmy. "Him and Joe Spence pulled out a little while ago. Either for town or the Circle 60. Most likely the last, for Leach has something he's going to tell Broderick."

Hitch Wheeler considered this while he built a cigarette. Then he tipped his head. "Trouble shaping up?"

Jimmy nodded. "Could be. Broderick's drifted cattle onto our Indian Mounds range. He thinks Leach is going to take that lying down, he's crazy."

A ghost of a smile touched Wheeler's lips. He took a couple more drags on his cigarette, then ground out the butt on his saddle horn. He lifted his reins, swung his horse. "I'll look Carlin up," he said briefly. "Obliged."

He rode away along the town trail until the ranch headquarters had dropped from sight beyond a roll of the prairie, then swung off at an angle and spurred his mount to a run.

In his law-office room, Mike Quarney faced Clint Brandon across the width of the big desk. Quarney's hatchet face was locked in inscrutability, now that he'd recovered from his first surprise at finding it was Clint who had knocked on his door.

He hadn't the slightest idea what had occasioned this visit, but he was under no illusion as to Clint's makeup, so he was ready for anything. He indicated a chair and took the desk chair himself. He used the old trick of letting Clint dangle for a little time while he selected a cigar with exaggerated care, snipped the tip off it precisely with a pair of desk scissors, then lit it carefully. Finally, with the smoke blooming in front of him, he put his narrow, masked gaze on his visitor.

"You said you had a good reason for coming to see me. Let's hear it."

Now it was Clint who took his time about answering, while he spun up a cigarette. Clint felt he had real weapons in the deal he was about to propose. He met Quarney's glance and watched the man's expression closely as he said, "First, a question. How much of Circle 60 is Broderick, and how much is you?"

Mike Quarney was a pretty good poker player, but Clint's abrupt question brought about a start of surprise which Quarney could not fully hide. Clint smiled faintly. "So there is a connection. I've thought so for a long time. Which means we'll probably be able to do business."

Quarney's veined cheeks showed a flush of anger. "I don't know what you're talking about, Brandon."

Clint leaned back easily. "I'm talking about that piece of range below the Indian Mounds."

Quarney had regained control of himself again. His face was blank. He took his cigar from his lips, stared it the tip of it. "It was my understanding, according to the word that's gone around, that Leach Carlin was the only man authorized to talk about any part, or all, of Hackamore. Don't tell me the authority out there has switched again?"

A faint touch of color ran through Clint's smooth checks. "This has nothing to do with any kind of authority. I'm just talking about a piece of range first, and after that about a piece of paper."

Mike Quarney lost himself again in a billow of cigar smoke. What, he wondered, was this slippery whelp driving at? What was the angle, the purpose? Was Clint just guessing at something, or did he know something? Was this just some sort of ruse to trick him, Mike Quarney, into admitting his connection with Circle 60? And what had Clint meant by saying they could do business, if such a connection was admitted? What about range, and what about a piece of paper? Quarney had the uneasy conviction that there was something here he should know about, but he couldn't for the life of him put his finger on it. He fenced cautiously.

"You're talking in circles, Brandon. If there's a point, come to it."

"I've already come to it," Clint said. "You heard me say a piece of paper. That's the point. It's a deed — a deed of sale. Covering the Indian Mounds-Steptoe Creek range. A transfer of that property from a fellow named Manuel Quesada to my father. All regular — all legal. Could it mean anything to you?"

It meant something all right. It meant plenty! Mike Quarney's mind was working furiously. It was jolting news, for he had never dreamed that Brandon had acquired the land by any other means than just moving in and claiming it, back when Big Sage Prairie had been all open range and the casual but accepted rule was first there, first owned.

It was one thing to move in and contest such a claim of prior use. A law court could be swayed in several ways in a case of that sort. But it was an entirely different matter if the other outfit could show an actual deed of ownership. No matter how this Quesada had established his claim in the first place, the fact that Brandon had bought the range and paid hard money for it — and had a deed to prove it — would stand as a powerful persuader in any court, for it was proof that Brandon had acted in good faith.

Mike Quarney's hand was being forced. He'd hoped to keep his interest in Circle 60 a secret for some time yet, letting Case Broderick be the front. Maybe he could still keep it more or less under cover if he handled this fellow Clint right. He could see that Clint was working up to some kind of a deal. Maybe he could handle the matter so that Clint's silence would be part of the deal. Quarney's voice went thin.

"You have this deed with you?"

"Hardly. But I've got it where I can put my hand on it any time I want. Let's come to the point. What's that deed worth to you?"

Quarney did not answer for a moment. Then — "You representing Martha Brandon, wanting to sell?"

"I'm representing nobody but myself," said Clint. "For some reason of your own, you and Broderick are hot after that Indian Mound range. I got no idea why you should want it, but it seems you do. If you had the deed it stands to reason that it would make your trail a lot easier. So — what am I offered?"

Clint was smug. He held the whip hand here, knew it, was using it.

"Why come to me instead of Broderick?" asked Quarney.

Clint smiled slyly. "It's generally the fellow who sits back out of sight who carries the real weight."

"You seem quite sure that I have something to say about Circle 60 affairs."

"Well haven't you?"

Quarney knew he had to come into the open. "Very well, say that I have." He went silent for a time, his eyes masked behind the smoke of his cigar. Damn that deed! It could ruin his whole carefully laid plan. The more thought he put to it, the more he realized he had to have that piece of paper. Yet it wouldn't do to appear too eager. Far from having any scruples himself, at this moment he had a vast contempt for this smooth-faced fellow across the desk from him. Here was as low a sell-out as any man had ever contemplated. It took an effort to keep the contempt out of his voice.

"Things would be easier for me if I had the deed," he admitted. "How about a thousand dollars?"

Clint laughed. "Let's talk sense, Quarney."

A flush of anger touched Quarney's gaunt cheeks. "Two thousand?"

Clint shook his head. "You're not even close."

"Three?"

Clint leaned across the desk. "Why drag it out? If you want that deed fifteen thousand dollars worth, it's yours. But not for one damned cent less. And," Clint added, "I want cash!"

The anger in Quarney swelled, staining his veined cheeks hectically. "Suppose," he said harshly, "I dropped a hint in the proper quarters that you were trying to sell out Hackamore, and by what means? Where would that leave you?"

Clint grinned mockingly. "Wherever it left me, it would also leave you without the deed. You can't scare me, Quarney." Now Clint laid on the whip. "I wasn't giving it to you entirely straight when I said I had no idea why you and Broderick are so hot after that piece of range. I still don't know for sure, but maybe I can guess pretty close. Could it have something to do with a dam, built down in the river gap below the Mounds?"

Quarney's hand shook a little as he took his cigar from his mouth. "I can't lay hold of fifteen thousand in cash just by snapping my fingers. It'll take a little time."

"How much time?"

"I think I can manage it within a week. I'll get word to you. You deliver the deed and I'll hand over the money."

"Fair enough," nodded Clint. Then he showed his sly, mocking smile again. "But there'll be none of this 'Won't-you-walk-into-my-parlor-said-the-spider-to-the-fly' business. We'll exchange compliments right in Billy Prior's store, some evening when the mail has come in. We won't advertise our business, of course, but the store will be a good place to play everything safe and cozy."

"Anywhere you say," shrugged Quarney. "I'll let you know when I'm ready."

A change had come over Mike Quarney. The stain of anger had faded from his face and there was something almost suave about him. A faint thread of uneasiness awoke in Clint. Had Quarney acceded to his demands too easily? Did the fellow have something up his sleeve? Quarney seemed to read the thought. He reached into a deep desk drawer and brought out bottle and glasses.

"A gentleman's way of sealing a deal," he said. "You'll find this as fine a rye whiskey as money can buy."

The drinks were generous and it was good whiskey. It burned away Clint's suspicions, and he knew a feeling of triumph as Quarney went with him to the door. Shove him out of the picture at Hackamore would they? He'd show them!

Slipping back toward the middle of town, Clint packed this thought with him and reveled in it. That drunk he'd been on had turned out to be the luckiest break of his life. Otherwise he wouldn't have been present on a late afternoon to listen at the door of the ranch office and hear several surprising things. About a deed, for instance — and some I.O.U.s.

Well, the deal was set by which he'd cash in on that deed — fifteen thousand dollars worth. Now to see about the I.O.U.s! Probably he wouldn't be able to get the full amount of them from Sam Desmond. But if he got half, that wouldn't be bad. For then he'd end up with some eighteen thousand, which was a lot of money in any man's language. With that much in his pocket he could travel a long way and do a lot of things he'd always wanted to do. With that much in his poke, he could say to hell with Hackamore, once and for all. Clint felt good.

Back in his law office, Mike Quarney poured himself another drink and his eyes burned with a sardonic light. That treacherous whelp Clint! It would be strange indeed if Mike Quarney couldn't out-scheme that fellow.

Sam Desmond's Square D headquarters

stood back toward the lower slope of the Warners and reflected the same physical sloth that had overtaken its owner. The ranch house was framed by several poplar trees. It was of two stories and had once been an imposing white. Now it was faded, a weary-looking gray, paint-peeled and weathered down to bare boards. There was a veranda across the front, set high enough to need a flight of five steps. The lower one of these was split and sagging, ready to trap an unwary boot heel. A pane of glass was broken in one of the second-story windows and plugged with a wad of rag. Out back, corrals and lesser ranch buildings were run down and decrepit looking.

Sam Desmond sat on the top step and watched Clint Brandon ride up. Desmond's eyes were bloodshot from too much whiskey and his pouchy face even more sagging and loose than ever. He offered no greeting to Clint, just sat there hunched and surly and looking much the worse for wear. Clint reined in, sagged sideways in his saddle and nodded.

"Hello, Sam. Was hoping I'd find you home."

Desmond stirred. "You found me," he grunted thickly. "What do you want?"

Clint looked him over, decided there was

no point in beating around the bush. "Little question of money, Sam. What do you intend to do about those I.O.U.s?"

Desmond's glance flickered and his pendulous lips pulled tight. "What I.O.U.s?"

"You know damned well what ones," said Clint, "those covering the money my father loaned you. Around six thousand dollars. Quite a chunk of money, Sam."

Desmond realized it would do no good to try to deny the fact any longer. He showed a glint of belligerence.

"If I owed that money to Dan Brandon, then I owe it now to Martha Brandon. Did she send you to collect?"

"No. But —"

"Then how do you figure it's any concern of yours? You're not running Hackamore. Leach Carlin is."

Clint reddened, his lips twisting in a quick spasm of anger. "That's why I'm talking to you now. Because I got a proposition to make you. While those I.O.U.s are in possession of Hackamore, then you owe Hackamore just about six thousand. But if those I.O.U.s were destroyed, then you wouldn't owe Hackamore a cent. I'll settle for half."

Sam Desmond licked his lips. "Half?"

"That's right. For three thousand I'll turn

the I.O.U.s over to you. Just a quiet deal between the two of us."

"Doesn't your mother or Leach Carlin know about them?"

"No," lied Clint. "But they will, one of these days. Only a matter of time before they'll go through all of Dad's old records, and when they do they're sure to run across them. And when they do, you can bet Carlin will be looking you up and calling for the money — all of it! But if you play along with me, you'll get out with half."

Sam Desmond licked his lips again. "You've seen the I.O.U.s? You can get hold of them?"

"Any time I want," Clint said. "I know where they are."

Desmond got out a grimy tobacco sack, built a bedraggled cigarette with none-too-steady fingers. "You'll have to give me a little time. Money's tight right now."

"How about a week?"

"A week!"

"BusIness is business, Sam," said Clint remorselessly. "And remember, at any time Carlin may get the idea to comb those records."

Sam Desmond stared straight ahead, his bloodshot eyes blurred with a dull hopelessness. Six thousand — three thousand! The figures tumbled about in his mind. Hell! Right now he couldn't raise three hundred to save his soul. Those cursed I.O.U.s — how they had haunted him! Brandon had never pressed him about them, and he'd almost sold himself on the conviction that Brandon had destroyed them. But he hadn't, or Clint wouldn't have known about them. Part of Brandon's carefully kept records they were, so Clint had said.

Desmond remembered the times he'd sat in Brandon's office and seen old Dan refer to some of those records in the closet in the office. Or add another to them —.

Desmond's glance came back to Clint, who was watching him with a glint of mockery in his dark eyes. There was a strong streak of cruelty in Clint Brandon and he knew no pity at all for this haggard man in front of him. Sam Desmond saw and recognized both the mockery and the cruelty and deep inside his sodden being a spark of anger flared and grew and he spoke bitterly with a long-denied honesty.

"I'm a washout, Clint. But by God, alongside of you I'm a man! You're about as low a whelp as I've ever known. You're a dirty, double-crossing rat! Martha knew what she was doing, all right, when she picked Leach Carlin to run Hackamore instead of turning the spread over to you. And to think that once I hoped to see you and Beth make a match of it. Now chew on this! You don't bleed me for one damned cent. When Carlin or Martha Brandon find the I.O.U.s then I'll talk straight to them and take my chances. But you — ! Get off my land — get off it, now!"

Sam Desmond lurched to his feet, a hand sliding inside the half-opened front of his grimy shirt.

Clint swung his horse a little further away, a hand dropping toward his gun. Sam Desmond started coming down the stairs, a strange, wild glare in his eyes that put a thread of ice up and down Clint's spine. Clint reined fully about and spurred away.

Sam Desmond watched him go, low, hoarse curses running out of him. But with the curses, the rage ran out of Desmond, too. There wasn't enough fiber in this man to hold onto any of the stronger emotions for any length of time, not even anger.

He shuffled around to the rear of the house and from under one corner of a low back porch brought forth a bottle. He held this against the sun, measuring the contents. He pulled the cork and started to lift the bottle to his lips. It was then that the idea struck him.

He held the bottle, half raised, while the idea took hold and grew. Why not, by God — why not! His lumpy shoulders straightened. A gleam, part desperation, part hope, drove some of the weary murk from his eyes. It was worth the chance — in fact it was his only chance. And if he could put it over, he'd show that damned Clint. He'd show them all!

He lifted the bottle all the way to his lips then, and drank deep.

CHAPTER EIGHT

The East Flank of the Warner Mountains was slashed by several canyons of varying size and depth. In the timbered and rock-ribbed fastnesses of these, creeks were born, tumbling the length of the parent canyon before breaking out into the prairie and working a more leisurely way across this to join the river. Most of them, somewhere along the course from mountains to river, looped past long, running meadows and in one of these, beside the waters of Antelope Creek, stood Case Broderick's Circle 60 headquarters.

It was a bachelor spread, with no frills about it. Just a few squat buildings built of logs brought down from the Warners, and a layout of corrals. Alders and willow clumps fringed the creek, but the buildings stood barren and in the open. Several horses lazed about the cavvy corral and others, still under saddle, were lined along the corral fence. At the lower end of the meadow some cattle were in evidence, with more dotting the rolling prairie to the south, where the main Circle 60 range lay.

Leach Carlin and Joe Spence came in on the headquarters from the north, pausing for a moment on the low lift of land above the creek. Joe Spence had his look at the place, then murmured, "Broderick's got company, looks like. Either that, or he's taken to hiring extra hands lately."

There was a left-handed suggestion of caution in Joe's remark, but Carlin pushed it aside with an impatient shrug.

"We're going in," he said bluntly. He gave action to his words by touching his horse with the spur and sending it on down the low slope.

Over at the door of the Circle 60 bunkhouse, Ward Dancy stepped into view. He caught the flicker of movement there on the north slope above the meadow, squared around and stared for a moment, then as Carlin and Joe Spence dropped from sight behind the creek growth, Dancy ran for the cabin which Case Broderick called his ranch house, sending an urgent call ahead.

"Case, hey, Case — !"

All the way over on the ride from Hackamore, Leach Carlin had been weighing the piling up of events since he'd taken over the authority of Hackamore. First had come Broderick's ultimatum and threat.

Then there had been that slashing knife in a dark hotel room. There had been a dry-gulch attempt that had gone only a little wide. And now there were Circle 60 cattle on the Steptoe Creek-Indian Mounds range. They were throwing it at him, throwing it right in his face; challenging his authority, his ability. They were forcing it down his throat.

Well, enough of that! He'd told Martha Brandon that you couldn't hold Hackamore together if you gave in on any one point. You couldn't defend any part of it unless you defended all of it. You couldn't be weak on one hand and strong on the other. Nor could you win any fight by just defending, while giving the other side the advantage of always calling the turns. You couldn't be negative, or the positive would swallow you up.

In the Prairie House that evening not so long ago, Broderick had made his threat, and he, Leach Carlin, had given it back. Trouble for trouble. Well, he'd meant it then, Carlin told himself, and he meant it now. There was a steadily rising temper in him that darkened the blue of his eyes. As his horse splashed across the creek shallows and drove through scrub willow to the open meadow beyond, Carlin seemed to tower in his saddle and his shadow lengthen.

The blind side of Broderick's cabin was toward the creek, with the door opening to the south, on the far side. Carlin and Joe Spence broke across the meadow and around into the clear before the cabin. Case Broderick was the only one in sight, and he stood in the cabin doorway, a shoulder point hitched negligently against the door post. There was a sardonic light in his cold eyes as he inclined his head slightly.

"Hardly a pleasure, Carlin," he said mockingly. "But not entirely unexpected. There's something bothering you?"

Carlin made swift survey of the layout, marking its apparent emptiness, and understanding the silent threat of this. Then he spun his horse to face Broderick and sat looking down at the man in the cabin doorway. His voice was harsh.

"Open your ears and forget the smooth talk, Broderick. You've made your move, it seems. You've pushed a jag of cattle onto the range below the Indian Mounds. So now Hackamore makes its move. You've just lost those cattle."

"So-o?" drawled Broderick. "Afraid I don't follow you. Maybe you'd better explain."

"That's Hackamore grass the cattle are eating. And Hackamore grass doesn't come free to you or anybody else, Broderick. Hackamore sets its own grazing fee on its grass. In this case it stands as a dollar a day per head. As fast as a Circle 60 critter eats up its worth, it will be rounded up and sold to satisfy Hackamore's claim. In about twenty days you'll have forfeited all title to those cattle. Maybe you follow me now?" Carlin's words ended on a note of cold sarcasm.

Broderick barked a curt, mirthless laugh. "Just like I laugh now, Carlin, any court in the land would laugh that sort of claim right out of its doors."

"What court, Broderick? The nearest one I know of is in Centerville, a long way from here. Takes time to get a claim set up in court, and a lot longer to get a decision. Also, any court is always willing to admit two sides to any question. Yeah, you've lost those cattle."

Case Broderick didn't show it openly, but this angle Carlin had brought up had jolted him. For it was one that neither he nor Mike Quarney had considered. Their primary thought had been merely that by throwing a sizable herd on the disputed range, they could establish a claim of possession. Such a tactic had been used before with success in some quarters. But if Carlin chose to go ahead with his flatly avowed intention,

191

Broderick could see where Circle 60 had indeed made a costly move. He straightened from his slouched ease, but still affected his attitude of nonchalance.

"One big hole in your argument, Carlin. That grass doesn't belong to Hackamore."

Carlin let him have it then, straight in the teeth. "When you say that, Broderick, you lie!"

That did it. It brought Broderick out of the doorway in a long stride, a gust of anger whipping across his face.

"You're just too damn free and easy with that word, Carlin!"

Broderick lifted his hand in a short gesture. From the doorway behind him stepped Duff Randall and Vern DeLong. Ward Dancy showed in the cabin door, stayed there. Frank Labine and Shep Bowen were abruptly in view over at a corner of the corrals, and from the bunkhouse came two more riders, strangers to Carlin. Hard-cased, both of them and like the rest, armed.

Joe Spence gave a little, grunting exclamation, swung his horse to face the bunkhouse and corrals. But Carlin stayed as he was, staring down at Broderick.

"What's this supposed to make me do, faint?" he asked contemptuously.

A flickering, wicked light had leaped into Broderick's eyes. "You could be surprised, Carlin. Duff — Vern — cover these two wise ones!"

Duff Randall was too thick and heavy of muscle for real speed with a gun, but the swarthy Vern DeLong was plenty fast. Carlin made no move toward his own weapon and when he heard Joe Spence's quick drawn, hissing breath, he spoke quietly.

"Easy does it, Joe. Let 'em wave their damn guns. Doesn't mean anything."

"That's what you think," rapped Broderick. "Get off your horse, Carlin!"

Carlin stayed as he was, his glance touching the men in front of him, one after the other. In Vern DeLong's dark, half-breed features he found no expression at all, save a black-eyed watchfulness. Here was a stolid, unimaginative sort who would cut a man down with no more compunction than he would know in stepping on a spider. Broderick was plainly exultant. Duff Randall was openly and savagely hating, and as he spoke now, his voice was still thick and hoarse from the lingering effects of a well-remembered blow to the throat.

"You heard what Case said, Carlin. Get out of that saddle — or be dragged out!" Randall stepped a little closer.

The two hard cases who had come up from the bunkhouse now moved around into Carlin's view. Broderick said to them, "Korb, you and Willsie get around and lift their guns."

Joe Spence said, "You call it, Leach. I'll go all the way with you."

"No argument, Joe," Carlin told him quietly. "They're just waiting for the excuse."

Korb and Willsie moved out of Carlin's view again, and then he felt the weight of his gun lift from his belt. Joe Spence said resignedly, "I thought I was too old to learn anything new. Know better, now."

Broderick laughed. "It's Carlin who doesn't seem able to learn, Spence. But he will, you can depend on that. He'll learn the hard way. He figured he was big enough to fill Brandon's boots. He isn't — not near. Duff, you said it right. If he won't get out of his saddle by himself, drag him out!"

Carlin could only guess at what lay in Case Broderick's mind, but the bleak realization came to him that whatever it was, it would be in no way pleasant. He knew a short gust of anger at himself. Here was another hand he hadn't played right. He'd let temper overrule calm reason and judgment. And he'd dragged Joe Spence into it with him. For Joe had suggested caution when they first came in view of Circle 60, and he'd refused to listen.

"You can leave Joe out of this, Broderick," Carlin said.

"Spence hasn't got a thing to worry about, providing he behaves himself. But you have. Get out of that saddle!"

Carlin shrugged and stepped down. Broderick jerked a nod and Duff Randall stepped around behind Carlin, holstered his gun and grabbed Carlin's arms, jerking them behind him. Broderick prowled forward.

"Now comes the lesson, Carlin!"

With the words, he hammered a heavy fist into Carlin's face.

Over by the corral corner, Frank Labine and Shep Bowen began to act very strangely. First they stiffened into immobility. Then they began to back up with slow, short steps, their hands half lifted. They backed clear around the corner until virtually hidden by the angling sweep of the corral fence. There a gun barrel slashed two swift, clubbing arcs and Labine and Bowen crumpled, one after the other, and lay senseless on the meadow grass.

Hitch Wheeler holstered the belt gun he'd used first to threaten, then buffalo the two, then lifted their own guns and threw them far and wide. He picked up the rifle he'd laid beside the corral fence and stole, swift and crouching, to the corral corner again. From there he could clearly observe the group of men in front of Broderick's cabin.

Over there, no one had noticed the actions, or disappearance of Frank Labine and Shep Bowen. All eyes were on the three central figures of Leach Carlin, Duff Randall, and Case Broderick. It wasn't pretty what they were looking at. Joe Spence was cursing in a thin, steady helplessness, and no one seemed to hear that, either. The sounds they heard were the spat and thud of Case Broderick's fists hammering into Leach Carlin's unprotected face, and the grunting effort Broderick put behind the blows.

Carlin wasn't taking it lying down. He was struggling madly to break loose from Duff Randall's grip, to get his arms free so that he could hit back at Broderick. But there was no breaking away from Randall's bull-like strength and the advantage he held. Randall's lips were pulled back in a grimace of pure animal enjoyment. Here was his vengeance, his chance to get even, and he savored every blow that Broderick struck as though it were his own.

Hitch Wheeler took it all in with a swift glance, then steadied his rifle across the corner corral post and sent a slug crashing into the front of the cabin, just above the door. The report of the rifle sent a thin rolling of echo across the meadow.

Ward Dancy literally fell over backward, getting out of the doorway. Vern DeLong spun around, the gun he still held gripped in his fist, lifting toward the point of threat. The action of Wheeler's rifle snicked cleanly as he swung the lever back and forth. The rifle crashed again and DeLong went down in a crazy sprawl, writhing and tumbling with a smashed shoulder. Hitch Wheeler's yell cut across the interval.

"Next man moves for a gun gets it center!"

Korb and Willsie had come around to face the corrals, but when DeLong went down, that decided them against any hostile move. Korb, in his turning, had swung closer to Joe Spence's horse than he realized and Joe, raging from what he'd been forced to sit and watch, slipped his right foot from the stirrup and kicked Korb savagely, full in the side of the head, Korb crumpled and Joe drove over him, landing full weight on Willsie's back and shoulders, knocking him flat on his face. Before Willsie could recover, Joe had hold of the gun Willsie had lifted off him. Joe swung it, hard, and Willsie, just starting to struggle, stilled into limpness.

Joe hit his feet, crouched and whirling, "Now, by God — we'll see!"

The crashing rifle reports, sight of Vern DeLong down and tumbling, blood crimsoning all the right shoulder of his shirt, made Duff Randall loosen his hold on Carlin and turn to face the unexpected threat. He saw Hitch Wheeler coming across from the corrals, saw the rifle in Wheeler's hand settle in line and the hard purpose in Wheeler's thin face. Randall froze.

Case Broderick, equally stunned, dropped the clenched fist he'd been set to drive into Leach Carlin's bloody face and started backing toward the cabin door. And then there was Joe Spence coming around to the side of him, gun level and ready. Joe was like some grizzled, snarling old wolf.

"Go for it, Broderick!" he urged. "Go for your gun — make your move. Just give me the excuse — !"

But Broderick had no chance or time to go for his gun, even had he intended to do so. For the bloody-faced man he'd been beating now came lunging and lurching into him.

Leach Carlin could hardly see. The world was a crimson haze in front of him, but the rage in Carlin was a black and destroying thing. Broderick tried to dodge aside, but Carlin's reaching hands got hold of him, pulled him in. There was a snarl Carlin's throat, a grinding, feral sound. With the first pull of his hooked fingers he tore the shirt off Broderick as if it were tissue paper.

He drove a lifting knee into Broderick's midriff that wrung a groan of distress from Broderick. He smashed his beaten head into Broderick's face and Broderick's nose caved under the impact. His gripping hand spread across Broderick's face and set down in a pinching grip which caved in Broderick's cheeks, forcing his mouth open, and letting out strange and inarticulate sounds. Then Carlin's free fist began to work.

He flailed it into the side of Broderick's head, knocking him back into the cabin wall beside the door. His left hand slipped down off Broderick's face and he jammed the web of it between thumb and forefinger against Broderick's throat, pinning him to the wall. Then, through that half-blind, crimson mist, he sighted on Broderick's face and swung his right fist again and again.

Anything that Broderick threw at him in return, Carlin never felt. For the initial punishment he'd undergone had beaten all feeling out of him. But Broderick was not trying to swing any blows. Fear was in him now, fear that was close to terror, because of this wild, destroying thing that was still a man, surging and beating at him. Broderick groped for his gun.

But Joe Spence was watching and jerked the weapon away from Broderick's clawing fingers. "No out for you, Broderick," yelled Joe. "You lit the fire!"

Joe was wrong. There was an out for Broderick. It was the measure of a man's strength and what he could endure. It ran out of Leach Carlin suddenly. The beating he had taken during those few short moments when he'd been held defenseless while Broderick's clubbing fists had smashed home again and again, and the last outpouring of strength in his raging attack on Broderick, had exhausted him.

His grip on Broderick's throat weakened and fell away. His final punch at Broderick's face fell short and he slid down to his knees, where he wavered back and forth in a darkening and reeling world.

Broderick himself shambling, tried to move toward the cabin door, but Joe Spence was there to push him away. Broderick slumped down against the low step. Joe Spence called harshly past him.

"Come out of there, Dancy — and come out peaceful!"

Ward Dancy came, his hands lifted. His mouth was slack and unsteady. Joe Spence took his gun, waved it.

"Over there by Randall!"

Hitch Wheeler had come up to within a few yards, now, rifle still poised. "I'll watch 'em, Spence. You do something for Carlin."

There was a bucket of water on a bench just inside the cabin door. Joe carried this over to Carlin, splashed some on his head and face. Carlin stirred at the shock, then mumbled thickly. "More of the same, Joe, more of the same!"

It brought him back, the wet and wonderful caress of it. It sluiced away the blood and comforted the bruises. It drove the thick mists from his mind and ran cold and wonderful down his throat and across his chest and shoulders. It seemed to quench the worst of the raging fire in his blood. It steadied him and got him back on his feet.

"I guess we can go home now, Joe," he said.

Hitch Wheeler caught Joe's eye and nodded. "I'll be along later. Maybe this is the first you knew of it, Spence — but I'm riding for Hackamore now. Carlin asked me to."

"You're a real hand, Hitch," said Joe.

He took Carlin by the arm, steered him over to his horse and Carlin, on the second try, made it into his saddle. Then Joe climbed into his own saddle and led the way past the cabin and across the meadow to the creek.

Hitch Wheeler let his glance run around him and smiled. The rider Korb, recovering now from Joe Spence's kick, had struggled to a sitting position, his eyes dazed and blinking. Duff Randall was surly and subdued, and Ward Dancy had nothing at all to say. Wheeler's glance settled on Case Broderick who, using the support of the cabin wall, had pushed to his feet again.

"Most run-out flock of would-be wolves I ever saw," jibed Wheeler. "You'll have to brew a stronger brand of medicine, Broderick. And when you report to Quarney, tell him my part in this, will you?" He laughed, soundlessly, then added, bleak chill showing in his eyes, "I'm leaving you now. But I'll be watching. Any funny moves and you'll get a lot worse than DeLong asked for. At that, he shaped up as the wooliest one of the gang. Remember — be good!"

Wheeler went away then, past the corner of the cabin, and on over to the creek. When the creek growth hid him, he hurried his pace up creek, to where he'd left his horse. In the saddle again and well beyond gunshot of the ranch headquarters, Hitch went swiftly up the low slope of the creek to the main run of the prairie. He rode a little straighter in his saddle than usual, and he thought, considering what had taken place over the past few days, he'd made a pretty fair start at earning his wages as a brand new Hackamore hand.

Back at the Circle 60, Case Broderick nursed his battered nose and face and gave harsh orders to Randall and Dancy, the only two able-bodied men about the place. Randall lugged Vern DeLong into the bunkhouse, took a look at the wounded shoulder and knew that only a doctor could do any good here. He unearthed a whiskey bottle and gave DeLong a heavy drag, then went over to report to Broderick.

Ward Dancy, going out to circle the corrals, found Frank Labine and Shep Bowen there. Labine was beginning to stir from the gunwhipping Hitch Wheeler had administered, but Bowen was still out. Dancy went back and gave Case Broderick his findings and Broderick cursed.

"Cussing," said Duff Randall bluntly, "ain't going to solve a thing. What do we do now? DeLong's got a mighty bad shoulder. Longer it goes without care, worse it'll be."

Broderick began stripping off the renmants of his torn shirt and ordered Dancy to bring a fresh bucket of water up from the creek. When this was done he washed up, put on a fresh shirt.

"I'm heading for town," he said. "I'll send Doc Persall out to look after DeLong. Rest of you sit tight until you hear from me. There's only been a couple of hands played in this game."

He went out and rode away. From the cabin door Dancy watched him go. "Maybe only a couple of bands been played," said Dancy. "But unless we play the rest of them smarter than the last, we'll end up with empty pockets. Don't know as I like my job too well, Duff."

Randall threw Dancy a hot glance, then spoke growlingly. "You signed on, didn't you? Well, now that you did, you stick. Don't try and go rabbit on us, or you won't last two jumps. I'll see to that personally. Now come along and help me get Shep out of the sun."

By the time he and Joe Spence got back to Hackamore, Leach was in pretty good shape again. His face was blackened and swollen and one eye was puffed completely closed. His head felt heavy, but the mists had cleared out of it. The crazy, wild rage had burned out, but there remained a still, hot ember of settled anger which would never fade.

Reaching the ranch, he saw that the Renfro buckboard had not left, so while Joe unsaddled and put up the horse, Carlin went directly into the bunkhouse and stretched out. He didn't want to face Martha Brandon or Dallas just now. All he wanted was a chance to rest and figure out the moves of the future. But anxious women were not that easily fooled or put off.

Before Joe could finish with the horses, Dallas came across from the ranch house.

"Joe," she demanded, "what's the matter with Leach? I saw him walk over to the bunkhouse, and he wasn't too steady on his feet. You ran into trouble at the Circle 60?"

Joe knew what was in Carlin's mind and he tried to figure some way out of this thing. But the clear intentness of this slender girl's glance was too sharp and penetrating to let any kind of evasion slip by. Reluctantly, Joe told the story.

He watched her face go white, then color up with furious anger. "That brute — that Broderick!" she cried softly. "Having Randall hold Leach, so he could beat him!"

Then Dallas was running for the bunkhouse. The place was empty, except for Carlin, and he lay still, his shirt stained with stiffened smears of dried blood, the lean brownness of his face lost under swollen, dark bruises. Dallas moved softly in and up beside his bunk. As she looked down at him her lips began to quiver, tears welled into her eyes.

Carlin opened his one good eye. "How did you get in here? Damn Joe anyhow. He didn't have to spread the word."

"Joe didn't spread anything," Dallas said. "I made him tell me. Your face — oh, Leach, I'm going to bawl over you — and, and you're not — not — !" Her words ran out into a little wail.

"Not worth it," he supplied. "Well, I know that. I'm a stupid, ham-headed fool and I walked right into something." His tone gentled. "So, don't you weep one little tear over me, partner." He reached out and captured one of her hands. "I probably look like the fag end of a massacre, but I'll survive. Now run along and don't bother your head over me."

"I'm running along," she told him, "but I'm coming back with hot water and things. I just won't have you lying there, looking like that."

She pulled her hand free and hurried out.

She was soon back, carrying a basin and a bucket of steaming water. Martha Brandon was with her, carrying several towels. They said nothing, just went to work on him. They washed his face, then put one steaming compress after another on his bruises. The effect was so soothing he began to doze, and then slipped off into a sound and healing sleep.

Pre-dawn's chill blackness held the world when he awoke. Around him in the bunkhouse men were sleeping. He lay for a little time, his thoughts growing clearer as he shook off the effects of sleep. His face felt stiff and clumsy, but his head was clear and renewed vitality made him restless and anxious to be up and doing again. He blinked up into the darkness, found that the compress treatment had reduced the swelling around his eyes so that he could open both of them again.

His restlessness grew and he threw aside the blankets that had been spread over him, sat up and fumbled about for his boots. He carried these out to the bunkhouse step, moving quietly, sat there and pulled them on. Then he straightened and moved out toward the corrals, stretching and flexing his arms and shoulders. The crisp chill of the early morning air felt good on his face, good in his lungs.

Over west the Warners ran their lofty bulk against the scatter of late stars. East, the

Nevada Hills were black shadows against a horizon just beginning to pale. In some far distance the lonely plaint of a coyote echoed thinly. Horses in the cavvy corral made a small stir of sound.

Carlin took it all in, with the responsive senses of a man to whom these things were flavor of life. This was Hackamore, all about him: this was the ranch whose affairs he must handle and build to betterment. Casting back over the happenings of the past twenty-four hours he saw fully the threat that hovered over these affairs; he carried physical reminders of it.

But he found himself measuring that threat now with a cool and uncomplicated viewpoint. No longer did he have to guess and wonder. Broderick had made his initial move — he'd thrown cattle on the range below the Indian Mounds. In the play he'd made down at Circle 60 headquarters he'd given vivid evidence of how far he was ready to go to make his claim of the range stick. The shadow boxing was all done with. From now on it was a toe-to-toe proposition, with no holds barred. And this fact brought its own brand of satisfaction. At least a man knew where he stood and what to expect.

Carlin leaned his shoulders against the corral fence, reached for his smoking. Then he stiffened, letting his glance run over the dark and silent bulk of the ranch house. He blinked and watched alertly.

Now he was sure of it. Beyond the window of the office was just the faintest glow, faintly yellow and flickering slightly. He pushed away from the corral fence and went across the interval, moving with prowling care. He came up softly to the window beside the office door, peered in.

For a long moment Carlin was very still. There was a man in the office, pawing through a mass of papers on the office desk. The flickering light was given off by a stub of candle, stuck to a corner of the desk by a gob of its own wax. As Carlin watched, the man tiptoed over to the closet, brought out another wad of Brandon's records, spread them on the desk. The candle glow brought out his features sharply.

Carlin moved past the window to the office door. This, he knew, had never been locked in his memory of Hackamore. It wasn't locked now. It gave easily as Carlin turned the knob and pushed quickly inside. His voice was low and curt.

"Just what's the big idea, Sam?"

Sam Desmond straightened up with a low, blurting gasp of dismay and with the same move his right hand darted into the open front of his shirt and came away gripping a knife with a ten-inch blade that glittered in the candlelight. He backed up a stride, the knife half lifted. Not until then did he seem to realize the identity of the man who had surprised him.

"Carlin!" he cried. "You — !"

In this short, suspended moment, Leach Carlin found the answer to one question that had been hanging at the back of his mind. And it twisted him up inside, for it laid bare one more facet of ugliness in the makeup of men. There was a weariness behind the harshness of his tone.

"Put that knife down, Sam! It didn't work before and it won't now. Put it down!"

For a short breath or two a glint of desperation shone wild and raw in Sam Desmond's eyes. Then it weakened and faded out and his lumpy shoulders sagged. He tossed the knife onto the desk, its fall muted by the mass of papers there.

"All right," he said heavily. "All right."

Carlin moved over, picked up the knife. "Why, Sam? Why that night in the Prairie House — and why this?"

Desmond fumbled for the desk chair, sank into it. His head sagged, he seemed to shrivel. He washed his hands dryly, over and over.

"When a man slides just so far toward hell and can see no way of stopping, he goes a little crazy, I guess."

"Those I.O.U.s, Sam?"

Desmond's head lifted a little and he stared upward at Carlin. "You know about them?"

"Yes, Sam, I know. Were they worth flicking a knife into me? You tried, didn't you?"

Desmond's head sagged again, bobbed up and down. "I didn't mean it that way to begin with. I was looking for you to have a talk with you. I was going to tell you about those damned I.O.U.s, and ask you to give me more time on them. Ace Lanier told me you'd gone over to the Prairie House to stay the night in town. He told me I'd probably catch you awake if I went right over. But then my nerve ran out and — and I went crazy."

Desmond began washing his hands again, twisting one over the other.

"Martha had put you in complete charge of Hackamore. That was a big jolt to me. I figured Clint would take over and I figured I could handle him, because he and Beth had become pretty good friends. But you — I was afraid of you. You got the reputation of being a rough customer, Carlin. I knew you were bound to find out about the

211

I.O.U.s, and would come after me. I tell you I went crazy. I'd been hitting the bottle pretty heavy, and that didn't help, either. Anyway — I got the idea — the idea —."

Desmond shivered and his voice faltered. He swallowed thickly and went on.

"I waited until I figured you sure to be asleep. Then I went into the Prairie House. Nobody was around. I scratched a match and took a look at the register and saw what room you were in. Then — then — well, you know the rest. Maybe — maybe you won't believe this, Carlin — but I'm glad I missed — glad I missed —."

"Glad about that myself," said Carlin, harshly dry. "You've been looking for the I.O.U.s — now?"

Desmond nodded. "I knew Dan kept a lot of records in that closet. I figured I could find them — get away with them."

He pushed up out of the chair, made an effort to square his shoulders. "I've made a hell of a mess of a lot of things, I guess. But damned if I don't feel kind of relieved, now that everything is in the open. And I'm sane again. It's up to you to call the turns, Carlin. Whatever you say goes. Only, I can't pay the I.O.U.s — I can't pay any small part of them. And I don't know as I ever will be able to. Lyle Barnard holds the paper on my ranch.

I got no real claim to a single damn thing."

Carlin watched Desmond levelly, seeing a man stripped of everything. Of his bluster — of everything. And knew a reluctant pity. A man was the way he was born. If he had it, then he had it. If he didn't, well — !

Carlin went over to the closet, located the little box, opened it and took out the envelope holding the I.O.U.s. He was remembering what Martha Brandon had said about them — about Sam Desmond never being able to pay them, that they should be destroyed. Well, she had spoken the truth about the chances of their ever being paid.

Carlin held them up. "Here they are, Sam. This will meet with Mrs. Brandon's approval. Maybe Dan would have felt the same way about it. Anyway — !" He tore the I.O.U.s into small bits. "You don't owe Hackamore a cent, Sam. Now you better get out of here."

Desmond's loose face began to work, words choking in his throat. Carlin headed him off. "No thanks necessary, Sam. I didn't do that for thanks. I'm not just sure why I did it, but it's done. Clear out, and take that knife with you. And when you're well out on the prairie, throw the damned thing away. You hear — throw it away! For if I ever catch you with it on you again — !"

"I'll throw it away," broke in Desmond, mumbling. "That's a promise — I'll throw it away. I never want to see it again."

He shambled out and was gone. The candle guttered and wavered in the draft from the door. Carlin stood long still and silent. He was wondering why it was that you could have such complete contempt for a man, and yet have pity for him, too.

CHAPTER NINE

Old Mert Downs had been cook at Hackamore for a long time. He was a little man, wrinkled with the years, and his whole concern in life was centered in his cook shack. Hackamore had never demanded anything more than this of him, for he was a good cook, sober and reliable. Now, though he wondered about the dark area of bruises on Leach Carlin's face, he said nothing.

Carlin was backed up against the stove, a mug of coffee cupped in his two hands. The warmth of the stove was pleasant against the morning chill. A new day was coming alive and riders began straggling over from the bunkhouse, intent on breakfast. They washed up at the bench outside the cookshack door, took their places at the long, oilcloth-covered table. They swung quick glances at Carlin, then looked away. Carlin grinned faintly and spoke with dry humor.

"It's turned into a rough game, boys. Take a good look at me and see an example of it. That's the way Broderick has decided to play, so that's the way it will be. Now then,

Circle 60 has thrown a sizable jag of cattle onto our range below the Indian Mounds. They figured that to be a smart move, establishing some sort of possession claim, just because they have the most cattle there. Hackamore is going to show them it was a poor move. Hackamore is setting a grazing fee of a dollar a day per head. Oh, that's a mighty stiff fee, I admit, but it's our grass so we've the right to set any fee we want. Right?"

Chick Partee, a lean, brown fellow with humorous eyes, chuckled. "Don't see why not, Leach. An outfit sure has the right to set any value it wants on its own grass. If the other fellow don't like the prices, he don't have to buy."

"Exactly!" nodded Carlin. "So that's the way it will be. If Circle 60 wants those cattle back, they're going to have to pay that range fee. If they don't come across with the fee, then as soon as the critters have eaten up their worth, Hackamore has the right to sell them for the amount due. I told Case Broderick that."

Carlin paused to empty his coffee mug. He put the mug on the table, wiped his lips with the back of his hand.

"I'm sending all you boys down to that range. You'll all pack rifles under your stirrups. You'll take along grub and blankets. You'll stay right there, guarding those cattle until I call you off. Joe Spence will be in charge. And get this. The cattle stay there. Nobody moves them off but us. If Broderick sends any men down there with other ideas, run them off and make it stick! If they have to learn the hard way — so be it."

Hardy Kress, an older, quiet man, spoke slowly. "Understand, Leach, I'm ready to ride just as far as Hackamore wants me to. But it would help to know that the Indian Mounds-Steptoe Creek range is, well — actually legitimate Hackamore range. There's some talk, here and there, that there's a question about it."

"Know what you mean, Hardy," nodded Carlin. "A good angle and I'm glad you brought it up. Hackamore has full and lawful title to that range. Dan Brandon bought it from a fellow named Manuel Quesada. I've seen the deed that proves it."

"Then," said Hardy in his quiet way, "Case Broderick will have one hell of a time getting his cattle back off that grass without paying the grazing fee."

A stir of excitement ran around the table and the crew was quickly through with their breakfast, eager to be on their way. Joe

Spence lingered a moment after the rest had left.

"You'll be ramming around by yourself, Leach, and you're the big one Broderick wants. He proved it again, yesterday."

Carlin ran an exploring hand across his bruised face. "Didn't he, though! Well, I got a lesson hammered into me, Joe. I won't make the same mistake twice. Take along plenty of gear and set yourself up a comfortable camp. But keep your eyes open. The squeeze is on Broderick now."

Joe went along out and then Mert Downs spoke a brief opinion.

"Reminds me of old times, Leach. When you gave those orders to the boys just now, I could have closed my eyes and believed I was hearing Dan. The language you used was Dan's language. Look 'em in the eye and be damned to them!"

Carlin went out and watched the crew make their preparations and ride away. Then he caught up a horse for himself and was saddling it when Martha Brandon came out of the office and crossed over to him. She stood looking at him gravely.

"After you went to sleep yesterday evening, I made Joe Spence tell me all about it, Leach. How much have I asked you to suffer for Hackamore? It's begun to haunt me."

Carlin's grin was almost cheerful, though a bit lopsided. "Just one of the bumps in the trail, Mrs. Brandon. I've been over such before. If a man never stops anything worse than a few fists in the face, he's got nothing to kick at."

She sighed. "I can see that I couldn't call you off now if I tried. Where did the crew ride out to, just now?"

Carlin told her, briefly. "That was Broderick's move. We countered it. Now we'll see what he tries next from his bag of tricks."

She glanced at his horse. "Where are you off to now?"

"Town. Couple of errands I want to do. Having another talk with Lyle Barnard is one of them."

He got into the saddle, then looked down at her. "Always pays to remember, Mrs. Brandon, that when our side of the argument shows rough spots, the opposition are having their troubles, too."

She watched him down the trail, then went slowly back to the ranch house.

In town, Carlin's first port of call was Billy Prior's store. At this hour of the morning things were slack and Billy was alone, puttering about. At sight of Carlin's face the storekeeper's glance sharpened and he shook his head ruefully.

"Seems every time I see you lately you show worse signs of hard wear, Leach. Who was it this time?"

"Broderick."

Billy grunted. "Real tough one, eh?"

"When the other fellow's arms are being held," said Carlin dryly. "Randall had hold of mine."

"My God!" exclaimed Billy. "Sounds potent. Tell me about it."

Carlin sketched over the affair, then added, "Lost my gun out there at Circle 60. Want a new one."

"With things shaping up that way, you'll probably need one. Help yourself."

Carlin went over to the gun case, looked over several Colt Peacemakers, selected one that he liked, found a piece of rag, perched on the counter and began wiping the grease from the weapon. The storekeeper watched him, gravely troubled.

"Hate to see it come to the need of that, Leach."

Carlin shurgged slightly. "It always does, Billy. These affairs always follow the same pattern. First it's words, then fists, then — !" He shrugged again. "If a man's halfway sane, he wants no part of such business. But what's he to do when it's shoved at him?"

"What he has to do — and go on living," admitted Prior. Then he added, "Pee Dee Kyne's got a new boarder."

Carlin tipped his head. "So-o?"

"Beth Desmond," said the storekeeper. "Signed on for a month, Pee Dee told me. Leach, I can't figure it."

Carlin worked at his weapon silently, remembering last night, and the man he'd found going through Dan Brandon's records. He remembered what Sam had said about Lyle Barnard holding the paper on his ranch. Was Barnard foreclosing, putting Sam and Beth out of their home?

He slid off the counter, thumbed cartridges from his gunbelt, loaded the new weapon and dropped it into the holster that had been empty up to now. He paid Prior for the gun, moved to the door. Over his shoulder he spoke gruffly.

"A man dies, Billy. Dan Brandon. And a whole damn range starts coming apart at the seams. Who says that men and what they stand for don't make events?"

From the store, Carlin went straight to the bank, where Lyle Barnard had just opened up. The banker gave smiling greeting. "Not time to have heard from my letters yet, Leach. What happened to you? Been using your face to drive fence posts, maybe?"

"That can come later, Lyle," replied Carlin gruffly. "First, what about the Desmonds?"

Barnard, startled, said, "All right — what about them?"

"You foreclosing on Sam?"

"Of course not. According to sound business I should have, long ago." Barnard pulled a cigar from his pocket, lit up carefully. "You know, Leach, the popular conception of a banker is a cold-blooded, hardhearted so-and-so. Perhaps it applies with some. But the coat don't fit me. This is my country. I like it. I like most of the people in it. As far as I possibly can, within the bounds of safety, I'll do all I can to hold any man together, if I think there's any worth in him at all."

Barnard paused, then went on. "To some, Sam Desmond has become a complete tramp. Maybe that's all he is, but I can't help feeling sorry for the man. So I'll carry Sam, and say nothing."

Carlin dropped a hand on the banker's arm. "My apologies for even questioning you, Lyle."

Barnard's cigar tipped upward. "You must have had a reason?"

Carlin nodded slowly. "I understand Beth

Desmond's moved to town — staying at the Prairie House."

"So naturally you thought I'd foreclosed." Bernard smiled faintly. "Leach, I never put a woman out of her home in my life. I never expect to. But if Beth Desmond has decided to play the lady in town, I think I know the reason why."

"I'd like to know, myself," Carlin said.

Barnard's eyes narrowed reflectively. "My friend, there are women — and women. Some are givers, others takers. Beth Desmond is completely one of the last. If Sam Desmond is broke today, Beth did her full share of greasing the way for him. You ever in your life see her in gingham, Leach? I never did. But I have seen her casually doing the town in a dress that cost more than a less selfish woman would spend for a full year of wearing apparel. Beth is looking out strictly for Beth. And now that Sam is pretty much down and out, well — !" The banker shrugged.

"That's sure laying it on the line, Lyle. And you could be guessing."

Bernard shrugged again. "I could be. But I long ago got over being blinded by a pretty face. Now, how about telling me what you bumped into?"

Carlin told him and as he listened, Barnard's face settled into gravity, then twisted with a sharp anger. "That's a damned, scurvy, cutthroat crowd, Leach."

"All of that," Carlin agreed. "But here's mainly what I came to see you about." He went on to tell of what he intended with the Circle 60 cattle. "I admit a grazing fee of that size is highway robbery, and probably any court of law would name it so and decide against it. What's your opinion?"

The banker chuckled dryly. "You didn't push the cattle on that range. Broderick did. An old dodge, trying to hog range by flooding it with cattle. And many times it has worked, where actual ownership of such range was open to question. But there is no question about this piece of range. It's wholly Hackamore's, bought and paid for. As long as it is Hackamore grass, you've the right, I'd say, to place any value on it you want. So now you got Broderick in a squeeze. He's got to move one way or the other. At a dollar a head per day, that's running into money — fast! And Broderick can't afford to lose that many cattle completely, particularly if they're not going to get him the range he's after. In your boots I'd look for fireworks, Leach."

"I'm looking," Carlin admitted. "Obliged for the time, Lyle."

Coming out of the bank, Carlin looked up street toward the Prairie House. He saw Beth Desmond step out of the door and take a chair on the porch. He paused long enough to twist up a smoke before heading up there. Beth watched him approach and showed him a smile that held both defiance and a slight uneasiness.

"Hello, Leach. What happened to your face?"

"Everybody asks me that," he answered. "I bumped it."

She was sleek and she had dark beauty, and the dress she wore was certainly not gingham. Looking at her, Carlin saw what Lyle Barnard meant. And he thought of Sam Desmond as he'd seen him, not too many hours ago in the Hackamore office, cowering and lumpy-shouldered, a man frantic with worry over debt, and driven by that worry to seek any way out — even theft and attempted murder. Hardness crept into Carlin's glance.

Beth stirred restlessly under the impact of that glance and something that was sultry and almost sullen came into her eyes and there was a curl to her lips which, in some strange way, coarsened her.

"There's a question in you, isn't there?" she said.

"Right!" was Carlin's curt admission. "You got a legitimate answer to it?"

She shrugged a handsome shoulder. "It's my life. I've the right to live it as I please. I just got completely fed up with living a run-down life on a run-down ranch. Anything wrong with that?"

"As long as you ask, yes, there is," he told her. "Sam never stinted you for anything while he had it, did he? Yeah, you helped him spend it. Now you're running out on him?"

She tossed her head. "Call it that if you want. I've a little money of my own. I can spend it as I wish. Now, if you're going to preach to me, don't. The role doesn't fit you."

He stood straight and squared in front of her, looking down at her with inscrutable eyes. Her glance slid away and there was the stain of impatient and uncaring anger in her cheeks. Carlin's voice ran low, as though speaking a thought aloud.

"How in hell could I have been so blind?"

He left it that way, swinging off down street to the Skyhigh. He turned in there and saw one man at the bar, toying with a solitary drink. The man was Hitch Wheeler, and at sight of Carlin he tipped his narrow head and showed his faint, sardonic smile.

Carlin said, "Hitch! I was hoping to run across you somewhere. After yesterday, I want to know what I can do to halfway square things with you. I didn't see you move in on that gang. About then I wasn't seeing anything too well, but Joe told me all about your part in the affair. Why did you do it, Hitch?"

The lank rider pushed his glass back and forth on the bar, staring at the pattern the moist bottom of it made. "You offered me a job, didn't you — riding for Hackamore? Well, I decided to take you up on it. I rode out there to Hackamore to tell you I'd made up my mind. Jimmy Spurlock told me you weren't there, that you and Spence had headed out for Circle 60. I thought I might as well ride out there myself, just to see what was what. When I got there, I saw what was shaping up, so I kind of moved in when they weren't looking."

Hitch lifted his glass, downed the drink, looked at Carlin and jerked his head significantly. Carlin followed him out into the street. Hitch was silent while he spun up a smoke, then he looked at Carlin with sharp intensity.

"When you going to learn your lesson, man? You're faced up with a bunch of coyotes who mean to go all the way. They won't

227

stop at anything. Why Broderick didn't give the word out there at Circle 60 to smoke you down the minute you showed, I'll never know. Probably he figured to, after he'd worked you over with his fists. Your life ain't worth a plugged dime. They tried to dry-gulch you once and —."

"How do you know they did, Hitch?" Carlin cut in.

Wheeler shrugged his high, gaunt shoulders. "I was there. I saw the try made. I'd been watching that jigger laying out on that point below the Indian Mounds. I wondered what he was up to. Then you and that Renfro girl came riding. With her sitting a saddle right alongside of you, I never dreamed the fellow would take a shot, chancing hitting her. If I had, I'd have nailed him to the ground with a slug. But he did try, and then by God, I missed him! Not once, but three or four times. Of course, he was getting out of there then like a scalded cat."

"So that accounts for those other shots I heard that day," said Carlin softly. "I wondered and wondered — . Hitch, who was it?"

"That's the hell of it," answered Wheeler. "I can't be sure. I wasn't close enough to be sure. I was back a good four hundred yards or better, which was why I missed him. After you and the Renfro girl left, I circled and cut the fellow's sign. He made some effort at hiding it, but I had no trouble reading it. His trail led back to Circle 60 finally. Now there's three out there at Circle 60 built a lot alike. There's Duff Randall, Vern Delong, and a fellow named Willsie. The hombre who made that dry-gulch try was one of those three. DeLong won't be in no shape to handle a gun again for a long time, so we can forget him. But the other two are still healthy, and may try again. Get it once and for all, Leach, it's turned into that kind of a game. I can smell more gunsmoke coming up."

"I hadn't offered you a job at the time of the dry-gulch try, Hitch. Yet you bought in on my side. Why?"

Wheeler stared away into nothingness. "Two good reasons," he said quietly. "First is, you've always acted white to me. You've treated me like I was a human being, not like I was some damn off-color skunk. Somebody else has smiled at and spoken fairly to Hitch Wheeler. I mean Mrs. Brandon. She's a great lady. She's Hackamore, now. She needs you to hold the ranch together. Before this thing is done, she'll need me, too. Which helped me decide to sign on when you offered the job."

"And that's Hackamore's good luck,

Hitch. Shall we ride out there now?"

"I'll be out a little later," said Wheeler. "One more thing I want to do before I leave town. Now, while I'm thinking of it, here's something else. Better keep a close eye on Clint. Because here's what I saw the other day." He told of Clint's visit to Mike Quarney's house, then added, "Quarney was Dan's enemy, and he's still Hackamore's enemy. He's backing every move Case Broderick makes, right up to his ears. So why should Clint pull a sneak visit to him? I'll let you guess at the answer to that, because I don't know it."

Carlin looked keenly at the man beside him. "So you're one Mike Quarney never fooled, eh Hitch?"

A harsh and biting bitterness was in Wheeler's answer. "No Leach — he never had me fooled. Well, I'll see you at Hackamore."

Wheeler turned away abruptly and started off, dropping a final word over his shoulder. "Remember what I told you about Clint."

"I'll remember," promised Carlin.

Carlin angled slowly over to Billy Prior's store, where he'd left his horse. His mind was churning with all Hitch Wheeler had told him. He was so intent on his thoughts that he was completely unaware of the approach of the Renfro buckboard until Dallas' clear voice reached him.

"The man's in some kind of daze. If he's added drunkenness to his other failings, I never will forgive him."

Carlin came around as the buckboard rolled to a stop beside him. Dallas was alone. She was bare-headed, her wealth of auburn hair spilling over her shoulders, her gray eyes shining with clear vitality. She looked absurdly young and Carlin remarked the fact.

"Put her in short dresses and a man would swear she wasn't a day over fifteen. Wonder if she'll ever grow up?"

Dallas sniffed disdainfully, jumped down and reached up to loosen the halter rope of one of the buckboard team. Carlin moved in. "Let me, youngster. Too high to reach for a little girl."

Dallas gritted her teeth. "I can reach high enough to swat you one, Mister Carlin. Only," and here she sighed, "I just haven't got the heart to add to the bruises. You're looking a little better than you did yesterday, Leach."

He grinned. "Feeling better, thanks to you and Mrs. Brandon. Now come on in and I'll buy you a lollypop."

Dallas muttered something under her breath, then marched up on to the store porch, her slim shoulders very straight. "It was a swell morning," she remarked at large, "until I met this man. Now he has me swearing."

"Let me put it my way," said Carlin. "It was a hell of a morning until you came along. Now I can feel the sun."

She turned and looked at him, her eyes going very soft. "Just when I think I'm all set to be really mad at him, the man says something that leaves me all wobbly inside. Be careful, Leach, or you'll have me thinking you really like me."

"Maybe the word is too mild," he drawled.

Hot color leaped into her cheeks and she looked away. She went still, staring. Up on the hotel porch, Beth Desmond was just leaving her chair, turning in to the hotel door. The color in Dallas' face drained slowly away.

"So that's it," she said tightly. "The beautiful one is in town, so the man rides in. Seems like he just can't get rid of the old lure."

She marched into the store before Carlin could answer.

After leaving Leach Carlin in front of the Skyhigh, Hitch Wheeler drifted south along the street a little way, cut into an alley and disappeared. A couple of minutes later he was climbing the steps to ex-Senator Mike Quarney's house. As he reached the top of the steps the door of the house opened to let out one Pete Busby, a frowsy, hang-dog-looking individual who hung around Modoc City and made a precarious living doing odd jobs here and there and running errands for an occasional dollar. Busby, startled, gave Hitch a quick nod and shuffled hurriedly away. Hitch watched him for a moment, then pushed open the door and went on in.

Mike Quarney was in his office, packing a savage frame of mind. It was the residue of the anger that had convulsed him the evening before when Case Broderick had come to him to report several things. The first of these had been word of Leach Carlin's stated intention concerning the cattle that Circle 60 had thrown on the disputed range. On hearing this, Quarney's first reaction had been the inclination to laugh. A dollar per day per head grazing fee! It was ridiculous.

But on deeper thought, Quarney realized that Carlin might very well put it over. Twenty days was no great length of time. The cattle could well be disposed of before court action could be brought into the argument and Quarney had no wish to have any part of this tied up with legal action. For he realized that several of the moves he and Broderick had contemplated wouldn't exactly stand clear-washed and white under the scrutiny of a fair court. In fact, the further Mike Quarney could stay away from any court of law, at least for the present, the better it would suit him.

He began to see clearly that what he and Broderick had figured a smart move was anything but that. For Carlin had come back with one a great deal smarter. And it emphasized one fact. He had to get hold of that deed of ownership that Clint Brandon had offered to sell him. So he and Broderick had made their plans about that.

Quarney and Broderick hadn't parted on very good terms, for Quarney had lashed Broderick heavily because of the way he'd handled Carlin at the Circle 60 headquarters.

"You had him dead to rights," Quarney had stormed. "You had the men there. You could have gunned him and Spence, and claimed they made the first play at gunsmoke. But no, that wasn't final enough for you. You had to work Carlin over with your fists, first. Yes, you could have gunned him and Spence, with no other witnesses about but our own men."

Broderick's retort to this had been to remind Quarney of Hitch Wheeler and the part he'd played in helping Carlin and Joe Spence out of the spot they were in.

"I always thought Wheeler was your man," Broderick ended. "It don't look like it, now."

This had been the final twist of the knife in Quarney and he was brooding about it now when Hitch stepped into the room, spurs tinkling softly. Quarney, seated behind his desk, came to his feet, his face convulsed. Rage crimsoned his eyes as he stared savagely at the gaunt, thin-faced rider. Hitch returned the stare unwaveringly.

"You!" snarled Quarney, his voice almost guttural. "You damned turn-coat! Just who you riding for, anyhow?"

"Hackamore," said Hitch quietly. "An honest job with an honest outfit. Seems to bother you."

"But you said that for five hundred dollars you'd take care of Carlin. Instead, you help him out — against me!"

"I didn't say anything of the kind," retorted Hitch. "I said I'd collect — get that — collect five hundred and more. I'm going to — from you! I'm going to collect and collect until I see you where you belong. In hell!"

Quarney tried to meet the cold impact of

Wheeler's glance, but he couldn't hold it. His eyes slid away.

"You'd take that stand against your own — your own —"

"Father," supplied Hitch grimly. "Do I always have to supply the word for you? Are you afraid to speak it, even here, with four walls around us and nobody but the two of us to hear you admit it? Well, I'm just as ashamed of the fact as you are, only twice as much. Gave you the horrors to even think of it in the old days, didn't it? In the days when you were Senator Quarney — 'Handsome' Mike Quarney, cutting a wide trail among the beauties of Washington!"

Hitch drew a deep breath and his voice grew harsh and cutting. "How you'd have liked to forget the girl you promised to marry and didn't — and the son you didn't want to admit! Yeah, the girl mother and her baby boy, out in a lonely western ranch shack. You sent a little money at first, didn't you — and then you even forgot about that. And so that girl had to carry it all alone. While you rode high and fat — and crooked — she worked like a slave to keep life in herself and her son. She stood the sneers and slimy talk of those who wondered who the father of her boy was — she stood all that and told nobody the truth, nobody but me when I was finally old enough to understand. When the heartbreak she had carried all the years finally became too much to carry, and she was dying — why then she told me."

Hitch's voice ran out into hoarse emotion. His narrow face was dead white, his eyes blazing pits. He was silent while he got control of himself again and his voice ran quieter.

"I was fourteen years old when I watched a couple of kinder neighbors bury her. Those same neighbors helped me carve her name in the wooden marker above her grave. Hetty Wheeler, that was her name. And Wheeler is my name. I'd rather be branded with a white-hot iron than carry yours.

"Well, I've been around quite a bit, just to keep reminding you. I've taken your damned money just to make you squirm, because I know how it twists you to part with any of it. And all the time I've been waiting for the big chance to help in cutting you down, cutting you right down to the soles of your dirty boots. Now Leach Carlin has given me that chance. He's offered me a riding job with Hackamore. I've taken it, and I'll have my hand in breaking you completely. I'm going to make you suffer like you made her suffer. Me, I don't count. But my memory of her does — above everything!"

In the face of Hitch Wheeler's impassioned words, Quarney had first tried to stand belligerent. But the whiplash of them was too much for him. He dropped back into his chair and there he seemed to shrivel. When Hitch finished and turned toward the door, Quarney half lifted a shaking hand.

"Wait!" he stammered. "I'll do the right thing — do right by you — !"

Hitch turned on him tigerishly. "Too late for that, Mister Quarney. I just told you that I didn't count. The time for you to have done the right thing is long past, buried in the years. You didn't give a damn, then. Don't try and tell me you do, now. I know better. It's just that your guts are shaking — you're afraid. Well, you've good right to be!"

Hitch left, then.

Mike Quarney listened to him go, listened to the fading clump of boot heels, the tinkle of dragging spurs. And when silence settled in completely, Quarney sat hunched, just as he was, for a long, long time. Then he stirred, got the bottle of rye from the desk drawer and gulped thirstily at it.

The wallop of the raw liquor took hold, driving some of the yellowish pallor from his sagging cheeks. The faded luster of his eyes quickened again to the old predatory glint. He took another drag at the bottle, got to his feet and paced up and down the room.

To hell with the past! This was the present and he had his plans, big plans. Things to do, old vows of vengeance to fulfill. Brandon was dead, but Hackamore was still there, to remind men of Brandon's worth. Yeah, Hackamore was still there to be torn down. And all his other plans — the dam, and the range the lake behind that dam would cover, and what possession of that range could mean to him in terms of money — !

As long as a man had plans and the will to work toward them — that was what counted. He could still make the present and the future good. To hell with the past!

Mike Quarney waited impatiently for a full hour, then went out and north along Bidwell Street to Coony Fyle's livery, where he ordered a buckboard hooked up and then drove out of town, heading for Circle 60 headquarters.

CHAPTER TEN

Out at Hackamore, Clint had slept pretty late. He got up, yawning, dressed leisurely, then went out, intent on breakfast. Over by the corrals, his mother had just climbed into the ranch buckboard, and Mert Downs, the old ranch cook, was handing up the reins of the eager team to her. Martha Brandon guided the team into a sweeping turn and drove off, and Mert went back to his cook shack.

Clint went down there, washed up and went in. Old Mert threw him a grumpy glance. "Hell of a time to be coming around for breakfast."

"That's what you're paid wages for, to serve food," Clint returned sharply. "Where is everybody?"

Mert rattled pots and pan before answering. "Your mother's gone to spend the day with Nora Renfro. Leach hit the town trail. Joe Spence and the rest of the boys are lined out to keep an eye on the cattle Broderick and his crowd pushed onto our Indian Mounds range. Going to cost Mister

Broderick a chunk of money to get those cows back — if he ever does."

Clint's interest sharpened and his tone grew milder. "How's that, Mert?"

Mert told him of the grazing fee Leach was setting, and then Mert gave vent to one of his rare, thin laughs. "Broderick figgered he was making a smart move, pushing that jag of cattle onto our range. Leach turned out just a little smarter."

Clint's face twisted in a sudden gust of anger. "Don't go praising him to me. One of these days he's liable to turn out so damn smart he'll smash himself and Hackamore, too."

Old Mert knew full well how things lay between Clint and Leach Carlin, and felt a secret satisfaction over the way Clint's nose was out of joint. But he had no wish to argue the matter, so he now kept his silence.

Finished with his breakfast, Clint went out into the morning brightness. Out to the west the Warners lifted, swimming in a powder-blue haze. There was a definite feel of change in the air, less of the settled heat, more of a bracing crispness. The good, vital days of fall, challenging those of the winter ahead.

The uplifting effect was lost on Clint, however. He saw the lure of the far distances, but they meant nothing to him. They never really had. He'd grown up, here on Hackamore, it had been his life as far back as he could remember. But it did not now, nor never had meant more than a representation of something that could be converted into cash money.

The beauties of far mountains, of wide sky, of long-running, empty distances, were completely lost on him. The spell of a land where a man might ride far, and know that special delight of complete aloneness, held nothing at all for Clint. Towns were what Clint yearned for, towns bigger than Modoc City, and money with which to buy ease and soft living. The moist sweetness of a season's first rain was not that to Clint — it was just wet discomfort. Clint had every instinct of a sybarite, though he wouldn't have understood the word.

He hung around, killing time for a couple of hours and had just about decided to saddle up and head for town, when he saw a rider come jogging in along the town trail, a rider who plainly wasn't too much at home in the saddle. It was Pete Busby, the odd-job man around Modoc City when he was sober enough to have some idea of what he was doing. He was that sober now.

"What brings you out here?" Clint demanded.

"You," answered Pete Busby. "Got a message for you. Mike Quarney sent it. Here!" Busby dug an envelope from a pocket and handed it over. Then, without another word, he reined around and headed back for town.

Eagerness leaped into Clint's eyes. He tore the end off the envelope, took out the enclosure. It read:

Ready to close that deal this evening. Seven o'clock at Prior's store. Destroy this.

Clint read it over twice, then scratched a match, held it to the corner of the paper, let the flames curl up until the heat touched his fingers, then dropped the remnant and watched it curl to black ash. He ground a boot on this, then turned and headed for the ranch office.

Exultancy gleamed in his eyes. Things were breaking right for him at last. Quarney ready to come across with fifteen thousand dollars, and nobody around the ranch besides himself but Mert Downs. And that old fool never left his cook shack if he could help it.

In the office, Clint opened the corner closet, dug down under the papers, came up with the little box. He put this on the desk and dug down into its contents. The fact that the envelope holding Sam Desmond's I.O.U.s was gone did not strike him. For Clint had given up all thought and hope of getting any money out of those. His last talk with Sam Desmond had convinced him there was nothing there for him. His only thought was the Quesada deed to the Indian Mounds range. He found this, tucked it into his pocket, returned the other contents of the box, closed it and put it back where it had been.

Then he went to his room, made up a small pack of personal things he figured he'd need in the immediate future, rolled these up in a denim jumper and left the ranch house with no more thought than if he was leaving it for just an hour or two, instead of for good. He crossed to the saddle shed, got out his silver-mounted kak, and then caught up his favorite horse from the cavvy corral, a big, solid sorrel. His saddle in place, he tied the jumper and contents behind the cantle, swung up and rode off.

From the door of the cook shack, old Mert Downs watched him go, wondering about several things. Wondering about Pete Busby riding in, talking to Clint a moment, handing him something which Clint had read and then burned. Wondering about Clint riding away now with a pack behind his saddle, just like he was leaving for a long time. Mert tried to figure the answers, couldn't pin down a single one, and turned back to his kitchen chores.

Clint held to the town trail for a couple of miles, then turned off it, headed along the winding bottom land along Tempest Creek and finally pulled up in an obscuring screen of scrub willow. Here he dismounted, ground-reined the sorrel, loosened the cinch, and hunkered down to take his ease.

An all-day wait lay ahead of him, but it was smart to play it this way, he concluded. If nobody saw him, then nobody would ask questions. He would hit town just at seven o'clock, as Quarney's note had specified. He'd drift into Billy Prior's store, conclude his business with Quarney in the brief space of time it would take to hand over one article and receive another, and then out and on his way. By this time tomorrow, he'd be far across the Warners, with fifteen thousand dollars in his jeans.

He rolled the amount over his tongue. It sounded good. It was good! If he'd been able to make some sort of deal for those I.O.U.s with Sam Desmond, the amount would have been bigger. But that damned, worthless Desmond! No matter. A man could still go a long way and see a lot of the good things of life on fifteen thousand.

Clint built a cigarette and lost himself in measuring the pleasures of the future.

Leach Carlin got back to Hackamore just short of midday and found Hitch Wheeler perched on the step of the bunkhouse. Hitch said, "Didn't expect to beat you here."

Carlin shruggd. "You know how it is in town. You meet up with folks. You do some talking. It eats up time. Let's go grub."

They went over to the cook shack, where Carlin said, "Hitch Wheeler is one of our boys now, Mert. Feed him."

Mert hustled around, put dinner on the table for them. He poured a cup of coffee for himself, sat down across from them. Carlin said, "I see the buckboard's gone."

Mert nodded. "I hooked a team to it for Mrs. Brandon. She's gone over to spend the day with Nora Renfro."

"Fine!" approved Carlin. "That's what she needs, to get out and around again. Clint show at all?"

Mert nodded. "Come loafin' in for breakfast, real late. Then, not long after, that no-account town bum, Pete Busby, rode in with a message of some sort. I see him give it to Clint; Clint read it, then burned it. Seemed to put some hustle in him for a change. He went into the house for a time, came out with some gear rolled up in a jumper, saddled that pet sorrel of his and headed out. Acted damn mysterious-like, seemed to me."

Carlin grinned. "You put in too much time in this cook shack, Mert. You're imagining things."

"No." said Hitch Wheeler softly, "no, he's not, Leach."

Carlin looked at Hitch swiftly. Hitch, meeting the glance, said, "In town this morning, I saw Pete Busby sneaking out of Mike Quarney's house."

Carlin considered soberly, then said, "We'll have a look around."

They finished their meal hurriedly, then Carlin led the way to the ranch office. They went through this and along the hall to Clint's room. The bed was tumbled and unmade and a couple of the bureau drawers were half open. A new sock lay on the floor.

"Looks to me," murmured Hitch, "like somebody might have sort of grabbed some things in a hurry — like they were going somewhere and expecting to stay awhile."

Carlin led the way back to the office, dropped into the desk chair, motioned Hitch to another. "You said you saw Clint make one visit to Quarney, Hitch. And you saw this Busby coming out of Quarney's house this morning. Then Busby shows here at the ranch with a message for Clint, who rolls some gear and heads out. Just about proves Clint has some kind of deal going with Quarney, but I'll be damned if I can figure what it would be. Clint hasn't got a lick of authority around here. Any deal he made with Quarney wouldn't hold a drop of water as far as Hackamore is concerned. No, I can't figure it."

"No way he could sell out to Quarney, then?" asked Hitch.

Carlin, twisting up a smoke, shook his head. "None that I know of. And if he'd been heading for town, either you or I would have met up with him along the way. Maybe he headed for Circle 60, though I'll be damned if I know why he'd do that, either."

Carlin got to his feet, went to the outer door and yelled across the interval. "Which way did Clint head, Mert?"

Mert showed in the door of the cookshack, waved a pointing arm. "Town," he called back shrilly.

Carlin turned. "You heard, Hitch? He must have left the trail somewhere between here and town. I got half a notion —."

"Shouldn't be too much trouble picking up his sign," murmured Hitch.

"You know, Hitch," said Carlin slowly, "it was Clint who cut the ground from under me before, here at Hackamore. He could have something cooked up to try it again. I'd like to catch him cold-handed in some of his damned scheming. Shall we ride?"

Hitch stood up. "Why not?"

They caught up, saddled, and headed out. The sign along the trail that was freshest was that made by their own horses, coming into the ranch from town. But there was another good set of hoof marks heading the other way. Carlin identified these from the saddle.

"Clint's sorrel. Big horse. Throws a larger track than most."

Hitch nodded. "This should be easy."

It was Hitch who picked up the spot where Clint had left the trail and they cut off across the prairie, following the sorrel's fresh-gouged tracks. They followed until the sign pitched off the low crest down to the Tempest Creek bottoms. Here Hitch Wheeler reined in, his alert glance taking in the brush-shrouded run of the creek.

"He follows the run of the creek that way, he'd hit the town trail again where it loops across at the shallow ford. But why would he bother to leave the trail at all, if he was heading for town? This thing don't look right. You stay put for a little time right here, Leach."

Hitch was dismounting as he spoke. He took off his spurs, hung them to his saddle horn. "I've done a lot of probling in my time. Picked up sign and followed it, just for the fun of it. I'll be back pretty quick."

Hitch dropped down to the creek, eyes on the ground. He turned west and disappeared past a point of scrub willow. Carlin slouched at ease in his saddle, spun up another smoke. He was completely baffled at Clint's maneuverings, but of one thing he could be sure. Clint was up to something shady. Carlin's jaw hardened at the thought. Martha Brandon had been so right in her estimate of this foster son of hers. There was, it seemed, no good in Clint anywhere.

It was near to half an hour before Hitch Wheeler showed again, coming back the same way he'd gone. As he climbed up to where Carlin waited, Hitch's eyes held a triumphant glint.

"He's holed up in a willow patch about half a mile along," reported Hitch. "Acts like he was just killing time, or waiting there for somebody. Still interested, Leach?"

Carlin nodded. "Plenty!"

"Come on," said Hitch. "I know the spot to do our watching from."

Hitch buckled on his spurs, swung into the

saddle and led the way down to the creek, across it and then up to the prairie crest on the far side. He cut south far enough to be hidden from the view of anyone along the creek bottoms, then turned west again. Presently there was a little side drift, dry this time of the year, but which would carry water in the spring of the year and empty that water into the main creek. They dropped into this, followed its windings until it began to widen above the creek. Here Hitch pulled up, dismounted and ground-reined his horse.

"He's down there just past where this drift hits the creek," Hitch murmured. "Come on."

There was a thin scatter of sage on the sloping shoulder of the mouth of the drift and they settled down behind this. "Grandstand seat," said Hitch softly. "We can see and hear everything from here."

Time began to run out in a slow, dragging wait. What stir of air there was lifted up from the creek, so they could smoke in safety, and this helped. The land held its big silence, of which all minor sounds like the twitter of birds in the creek growth were a part.

Hitch Wheeler ground out the butt of his cigarette, leaned his shoulders back against the slope of the bank, tipped his hat forward over his eyes. He was utterly still in a complete relaxation. He might have been asleep, but Carlin knew he wasn't.

Carlin studied that lean, hard-pulled face. There was no cynical cast to it now, but in the lines about the mouth there was a settled bitterness. It was the face of a man to whom life had been anything but kind. It was Carlin's thought that here was a man who had known the lash of injustice and who had built a hard, protective shell about himself. Here was no real depravity, but rather a taciturn, sardonic strength, fashioned from the rigors of life as he had known it. In this moment, Leach knew a deepening liking and respect for Hitch Wheeler.

The afternoon ran out. The sun dipped toward the Warners, touched the tip of Hardin Peak and laid a gilded mantle across the mountain's massive shoulders. Down in the creek bottom there was the stir of movement, the rustle of brush pushed aside and then Clint rode into view, keeping to the creek bottom for only a little way before setting his sorrel to climb up to the northern level of the prairie.

Hitch Wheeler, who hadn't moved a muscle in the past two hours, was instantly alert. He and Carlin got their horses, and with Clint gone from sight beyond the roll of the prairie, rode down and across the creek and up the other side.

The lengthy wait had put an edge of sharp impatience in Clint Brandon. Also a little thread of nervousness. His mind ran ahead to what it would be like in Billy Prior's store. He hoped there wouldn't be too many people around, just enough to furnish split attention, so that any brief interchange between himself and Mike Quarney would go unnoticed.

What if the bundle of money Quarney handed him didn't add up to fifteen thousand! Certainly he couldn't take time out to count it, there in the store. Maybe it would have been smarter if he'd arranged the meeting in Quarney's house, after all.

Clint swung his shoulders angrily. What the hell! He held the whip hand, didn't he? Quarney wanted that deed, didn't he. And wanted it bad. Just how bad was proven by the fact that instead of a week, Quarney had rounded up the money in considerably less time. Yeah, he'd pull Quarney out of the store. They'd slip off to some other place, where he could count the money and make sure of the amount before he handed over the deed.

Clint built a smoke, feeling better about things as he hastened the jog of the sorrel.

The sun slid from sight and the cool, blue tides of early dusk began to flow. Down the trail ahead of Clint, two riders hove into view, heading toward him. Clint eyed them warily, trying to identify them, saw them finally as strangers.

They rode with an easy unconcern and as Clint came up to them, reined out to give him his half of the trail. But through slanted eyes one of them was watching carefully, staring at Clint's silver-mounted saddle. Abruptly he rapped harsh words.

"Our man, Willsie!"

As he spoke, the fellow spun his horse on a dime, throwing it across the trail so abruptly that Clint's sorrel half reared to avoid collision. The second rider, passing Clint, swung in behind him. It was a trap and it had closed, tight!

For a moment Clint was too startled to speak, then his words broke out, high and thin.

"What in hell is this? What — ?"

"You're Clint Brandon," broke in the rider in front. "You got something we want. Hand it over!"

"I don't know what you're talking about."

"Hell you don't! Something you were going to sell to Mike Quarney. Only, your price was too high. Come across with that deed!"

It hit Clint all of a sudden, then. Quarney had double-crossed him after all! He'd ridden right into this —.

Unconsciously Clint touched a hand to the pocket that held the deed. If he lost that he lost everything. A blind and crazy desperation shook him. He hauled hard at the reins to swing the sorrel wide, dug in the spurs.

The sorrel answered, spinning, lunging, snorting, getting into full running stride with the first jump. A curse followed Clint, and then the flat, hard cough of a gun.

Smashing force hit Clint between the shoulders, driving him far forward over his saddle horn. There was no particular pain, just a great, terrifying numbness which took all his strength away. He rocked twice from side to side, then poured limply out of the saddle. The sorrel, with the silver-mounted saddle empty, raced away.

Willsie, reeking gun still half lifted, said coldly, "The crazy, damn fool!"

Korb, who had blocked the trail in front of Clint, swung from his saddle and ran over to Clint's sprawled figure. He had marked Clint's betraying move toward a certain pocket just before his desperate try at a getaway, so he knew what pocket to search. He had just got his fingers on the contents of that pocket when Willsie yelled in wild alarm.

"Coming in — two riders! Let's get out of here!"

Leach Carlin and Hitch Wheeler had been keeping Clint in sight, not by following the main trail openly, but by using the partial shelter of one of the low rolls of prairie which roughly paralleled the trail. They had closed up to within a couple of hundred yards when they marked the approach of the two strange riders. They had slowed then, watching this.

They were too far away to hear anything of the exchange of words, but they saw all too clearly the swift and savage sequence of events that followed. They saw Clint make his try at a getaway, they saw the gun's pale flash and heard its report. And they saw Clint go down.

Carlin, a gusty, explosive curse breaking from his lips, was first across the low roll of the prairie, spurring savagely. Hitch Wheeler was close after him for a few jumps, then, as Willsie's yell of warning echoed, Hitch hauled up his facing mount, jumped to the ground and dragged his rifle from its saddle boot. He spoke harshly, to no one in particular.

"They might outrun our broncs. They can't outrun this!"

He dropped to one knee, swinging the lever of the gun, jacking a cartridge from magazine to barrel chamber. Willsie, after yelling his warning, swung his horse to face the hard, pounding charge of Leach Carlin. Flame and report spat from Willsie's gun, once — twice! But the range was long for a belt gun, too long, and Willsie's lead hit nothing.

The light was fading, but Hitch Wheeler was wise in such things. He held low, just where man and mount blended into one bulk. At the rifle's sharp, ringing challenge Willsie was fairly lifted out of his saddle.

Now Korb was racing for his horse. A slug from Hitch's rifle dug into the prairie sod under the animal's belly, spattering fragments of earth. The horse, stung and spooked, snorted, kicked, and went lunging off, just before Korb's reaching hand could catch its rein. Cursing, Korb ran after it for a few steps, then, realizing he had no chance there, he whirled and darted toward Willsie's mount.

Here, too, he had no success, for the animal, edgy from the shot that had knocked

Clint from his saddle, and from the two shots its rider had thrown at Leach Carlin, shied wildly away from the lifeless bulk that had rolled off its back. And when Korb ran at it, it shied still further away.

Leach Carlin was cutting down the interval, fast! He had pulled his gun as he first started to close in. At a distance of some seventy-five yards he threw a shot, missed, and held his fire for a more certain range. Korb, caught afoot, settled himself in a cornered crouch.

His gun began to blare. But he could not put his full attention on that bulk of rider and horse thundering down upon him. For there was that other one — the one with the rifle, the one who had cut Willsie from the saddle. This split concern did not help Korb's shooting any. His first two shots were wild. His third cut a wisp of hair from the tossing mane of Carlin's horse. And then, at less than fifty yards, Carlin fired his second shot. It was chancing and went low, but not low enough to miss entirely. It smashed into Korb's left foot, jerking the foot from under him, letting him down in a sidelong sprawl. Before Korb could recover, the charging bulk of man and horse was right on top of him. Korb threw up an arm in what might have been either a gesture of supplication or an instinctive warding-off move. In either event it did not matter. For Carlin's next slug, thrown almost straight down as he thundered by, drove into the center of Korb's chest.

Carlin set his horse up in a rearing, sliding halt, spun it around, gun high and ready to chop down with another shot. But Korb was just a still and flattened blur against the darkening earth. So Carlin set his mount lunging over to where Clint lay, jumped from his saddle and dropped to his knees beside Clint.

Clint was face down, huddled in a way that told its own story. Carlin didn't even have to touch him to know it was no use. Carlin stayed as he was for a long moment, thinking not of Clint, but of Martha Brandon. How could he bring this one more sorrow to that woman's door?

The rattle of hoofs brought Carlin back to his feet. It was Hitch, racing up. Hitch said, "Dead?"

Carlin nodded, numbly.

Hitch said, "If it'll be any consolation, we more than evened up for him."

He swung down, prowled over to Willsie, then to Korb. As he came back toward Carlin, a pale gleam against the earth caught his eye. He scooped it up, peered at it.

"Leach," he said, "maybe this means something."

Carlin took the folded paper automatically, glanced at it, then peered closer. "Scratch a match, Hitch," he said harshly.

In the brief, flickering glow, Carlin saw what it was that he held. It was the Quesada deed to the Indian Mounds-Steptoe Creek range.

"So!" he exploded. "So that's it!"

"Then it does mean something?" questioned Hitch.

Carlin nodded wearily. "It means plenty!" He swung a glance at Clint, who seemed to be sinking into the earth, for darkness was claiming everything now. True to his make-up, Clint had been working toward the big sell-out. Carlin turned back to Hitch.

"You're entitled to know, Hitch," he said, quieter now. So then he told Hitch of the deed.

Hitch whistled softly. "Korb and Willsie — Broderick's men. Which meant they were Mike Quarney's men, too. They met Clint here and were set to take the deed away from him. They wouldn't have known anything about the deed unless Broderick or Quarney had told them. They knew Clint would be coming down this trail and they knew he had the deed with him."

Carlin nodded. "It goes further than that. It goes back to the day you saw Clint make that visit to Quarney's house in town. It goes back to Pete Busby riding out to Hackamore with a message for Clint. The fact that Clint laid out all afternoon along the Tempest Creek bottoms makes sense now. He didn't want to be seen in town until after dark, which meant he had arranged a meeting with somebody."

"Mike Quarney," said Hitch bitterly. "It would have to be with Mike Quarney. I wonder how much Quarney had promised Clint he'd pay for the deed — while never meaning a word of it, no more than he ever meant a promise in his life?"

Carlin swung his head, wondering at that bitterness in Hitch's tone. "You think that was the way of it, Hitch?"

"How else could it have been? You say Broderick and Quarney are out to establish a claim to that range below the Indian Mounds. They threw a bunch of cattle onto the range for that purpose, didn't they? Well, they wouldn't have a chance to make that claim stick so long as this deed was safe with Hackamore. I wouldn't know whether Quarney approached Clint about the deed, or if it was the other way around, but it's plain enough that some kind of deal for it was on between them. And whatever Quarney promised Clint for the deed was

261

sucker bait, nothing more. For Quarney had those two yonder out to waylay Clint and take the deed away from him. Clint fell for the bait and all he got out of it was a bullet in the back. That — that Quarney!"

"You seem," said Carlin pointedly, "to know Mike Quarney's makeup pretty well, Hitch."

Hitch stood very quiet for a long, long moment. Then he spoke bleakly.

"I ought to. He's my father. Only — he promised to marry my mother, and didn't."

A blow in the face couldn't have jolted Leach Carlin more than did these low, bitter words. They answered every question he'd ever had in his mind about Hitch Wheeler. The footloose, apparent aimlessness in life. That sardonic half smile at life and all the empty pretenses it set up. That carved, set bitterness in Hitch's face when in repose. Carlin dropped a hand on Hitch's arm.

"You're a damned big man in my eyes, Hitch — and always will be."

Hitch said, "Only three people in the world know. You, myself, and Quarney."

"Only three will ever know," said Carlin. He hesitated a moment, then added, "This means you won't be riding for Hackamore for a while, Hitch."

Hitch came around quickly. "Why not?"

"Because of what you've just told me — but not in the way you're thinking. You know what I've got to do now, Hitch. I've got to smash Quarney and Broderick completely. I'm going to. I'm going to run those two off this prairie, or put them six feet under it. And I can't expect you to be part of Hackamore while I do it."

Hitch laughed harshly, mirthlessly. "Why do you think I agreed to sign on with Hackamore in the first place? I had several reasons. Put it that I like you. Put that I've always wanted to be part of a sound, square ranch. And put it finally that I want to have a hand in breaking Mike Quarney, in tearing down his damn house of crooked cards, in making him suffer at least a little of what he caused my mother. Leach, I don't owe Mike Quarney a damned thing!"

Hitch shook himself. "Come on. We got things to do."

CHAPTER ELEVEN

Bois Renfro's pipe was a black, battered, odoriferous thing, and he knew from experience that his wife did not appreciate the smell of it in her house. So Renfro had fallen into the habit of taking his after-supper smoke out by a corner of the corrals. He was out there now, hunkered on his heels, watching the slow wheel of the stars and measuring the oncoming impact of the advancing season by the night wind pushing against his weathered cheeks. He heard the thump of hoofs and straightened to his feet, alert at the approach of two riders.

Leach Carlin's voice came in. "That pipe of yours is a dead giveaway, Bois. What a fumigator!"

Renfro chuckled. "Got to have my evening smoke, but Nora won't let me take it in the house." Then his tone sobered. "You're riding a little late, Leach. A reason?"

"Plenty! Clint Brandon is dead. And —."

"No!" cut in Renfro. "My God — how — where — ?"

"Couple of Circle 60 riders did for him.

Too long a story to tell now, Bois. You'll get it all, later. Mrs. Brandon doesn't know about it. She won't, until tomorrow. Here's why I stopped by. It's going to be a tough chore, telling her. And after she knows it would help a lot if, well — if Mrs. Renfro and Dallas could be on hand. You'll have to tell them, of course. So if they'd show at Hackamore tomorrow around noon. Think you can manage it?"

"Sure I can," growled Renfro. "Glad to. Anything else I can do to help?"

"That'll be enough."

"I'm thinking of Martha," said Renfro. "First Dan, and now Clint. How rough can life get for some?"

"If a man asked himself that question for a hundred years, Bois, he still wouldn't know the answer. Thanks."

Before Bois Renfro could think of another thing to say, Carlin and Hitch Wheeler rode on.

Renfro stared after them, then knocked the dottle from his pipe on a corral post, braced himself and went over to the ranch house, hating to bring this latest word of tragedy into that bright and warm interior.

From the Renfro place, Carlin and Wheeler set a fast pace, pushing their horses through the chilling night. In time they saw the dark, rounded bulk of the Indian Mounds lifting on either hand as they paralleled the run of the river. And a little further on they picked up the shortspread radiance of a campfire. Almost at the same moment, sharp challenge came at them from night's gloom off to one side. It was Jimmy Spurlock's voice.

"Name yourselves!"

"Carlin, kid, and Hitch Wheeler. Come on along with us."

There was the creak of saddle leather and then Jimmy moved up to them. "Something wrong, Leach?"

"Yeah. You'll hear about it when I tell the others."

Joe Spence had picked a good spot for the camp. He and a couple of others were lounging on their blankets by the fire. They came to their feet as Carlin and Hitch and Jimmy Spurlock rode up to the glow of the flames. Joe had his glimpse of Carlin's face as Carlin came closer to the fire.

"Something's wrong," said Joe. "What is it, Leach?"

"Where's the rest of the crew?" Carlin asked. "On guard?" Then, as Joe nodded, he added, "Bring them in. This is for everybody to hear. Any coffee left in that pot?"

Joe looked at Jimmy Spurlock. "Go bring

the others in, kid."

He stirred the fire up a bit, tucked the coffee pot closer to the flames, brought out a couple of cups and plates, scooped beans from a pot and poured coffee. Carlin and Hitch Wheeler hunkered by the flames, ate and drank hungrily.

Jimmy Spurlock was soon back, bringing in the other guards. They gathered around, building smokes, their eyes reflecting the question in their minds. Carlin drained the last of his coffee, let his glance run through the whole silent circle.

"First," he said, "Hitch Wheeler is one of us, now — and will stay so. Second, Clint's dead. Two Circle 60 riders killed him."

It jolted them, this did, brought their heads up, put a hard and startled flare in their eyes. Joe Spence rapped a hard question.

"Which two?"

"Those two hard-case strangers you and I saw out at Circle 60. Korb and Willsie was what Broderick called them."

"But why? What — ?"

"You'll know all about it, in time," Carlin cut in. "But right now we got things to do. I can add that Korb and Willsie got like medicine. Hitch and I saw to that. It doesn't stop there. We're all heading for Broderick's layout, now!"

Carlin got to his feet, spinning up a cigarette. In the flickering firelight reflection his face showed bleak and tautly cut, his eyes brooding and shadowed.

"They threw cattle onto this range. We coppered that bet. Now they've killed Clint. We do more than copper that move. They've made it plain that there's not room on this prairie for Hackamore and Circle 60 at the same time. It's not Hackamore that moves off! Well, any questions?"

They pondered it silently. Clint was dead and, aside from the jolting impact of this as a fact, there was, in all honesty, little real regret in them. For they had known Clint and knew his worth — or lack of it. But Clint was a part of Hackamore, and that was different. A blow against Hackamore was a blow against all of them. Hardy Kress shrugged, and in his even, quiet way that was far more significant than any amount of loud-voiced anger, spoke for all of them.

"Let's ride!"

Carlin said, "Douse the fire and leave your extra gear here. It'll keep."

Mike Quarney had returned from Circle 60 to town an hour before sunset. Just at dusk, Case Broderick rode in with Duff Randall. These two kept clear of Bidwell Street, circling well around and coming up behind

Quarney's house. They left their horses there and Quarney let them in by the back door.

Broderick asked, "Any word from Korb and Willsie yet?"

Quarney shook his bony head. "Too early yet."

They went into Quarney's office. Quarney had the shades pulled down here, and the lamp on the desk was turned low. Quarney and Broderick took chairs, while Duff Randall squatted on his heels against the wall.

Outside the usual twilight quiet held the town. Then Randall tipped his head and listened. "Stage coming in," he said briefly.

Randall's ears and the sound they read, jibed. The stage went through its usual routine of stopping at Billy Prior's store to toss down the mailbag, then rolling on to Coony Fyle's stable, where the team was unharnessed. After which the stage whip, Swing Benson, stumped along up to the hotel, where he met Lyle Barnard just coming out. Swing pulled a yellow envelope from his pocket.

"Station agent at Centerville asked me to hand this to you personally, Lyle. It came in over the railroad wire."

The banker tore open the envelope, tipped the enclosed telegram up so he could read it by the pour of light reflecting from the hotel door. He read it over twice, smiled, and nodded.

"Obliged, Swing. This little service on your part earns you a drink when I see you in the Skyhigh, later."

"I'll take the drink," said Swing. "But not just because I did you a little favor."

Dusk faded out before the sweep of full dark. Over east, above the Nevada Hills, the first stars set up their deepening glitter. A little wind pushed down Fandango Canyon and out across the flats, carrying the bite of mountain heights in its chilling breath. Lyle Barnard's stride was brisk as he angled along to Billy Prior's store.

In Mike Quarney's office a small germ of tension began to hang in the air. Quarney and Broderick both showed the effect of it in their restless stirrings. But Duff Randall stayed utterly still, a cigarette stub hanging from his heavy underlip. This man was too thick and unimaginative to be affected by any mere nuance of thought. His channels of reasoning were ponderous and wholly realistic. Time enough to consider any possibility when it was right there in front of him, where he could see or feel it.

Quarney pulled a heavy, gold-case watch from a vest pocket, glanced at it. "He was supposed to meet me at Prior's store at seven," Quarney said thinly. "Nearly that, now. You think Korb and Willsie might have missed him?"

"Not if he came in by the regular Hackamore trail," answered Broderick. "There's always the chance, of course, that he'd come into town from some other angle, not wanting to advertise his business to anyone. He's just sly enough to think up some trick like that."

Quarney cursed softly at the thought. "We'll have to think up another angle, and quick, if he does. Else we'll scare him off." Quarney considered a moment, then looked at Randall.

"Duff, take a turn up and down the street, especially around Prior's store. See if you can get a line on Clint Brandon. Go out the back way."

Randall nodded, pushed to his feet and went out at his heavy-legged, thrusting stride. When he had gone, Quarney produced bottle and glasses.

"That fellow's a damned clod — ninety per cent pure animal."

Broderick shrugged. "Useful, though. Does as he's told and asks no questions. He's got one weak angle. Like most thick-headed ones, he's superstitious. He doesn't realize it himself and wouldn't recognize the word. But he is. He's brooded a lot over missing that dry-gluch try at Carlin down below the Indian Mounds. And if I'd let him, he'd have gunned Carlin from the window of the ranch cabin when Carlin and Joe Spence rode in on us."

"Smarter than you were, there," snapped Quarney acidly.

Broderick reddened slightly, downed his drink. Wiping a hand across his lips he said, "That would still have been taken care of if that damned Hitch Wheeler hadn't come up and bought in out of nowhere. There's something I just can't figure. Why would Wheeler be tied in with Hackamore and bucking us?"

Quarney's eyes veiled. "Hired to, I suppose," was his abrupt reply. "In any case, Carlin and Wheeler both will be taken care of — in time. Right now, all I want is for Korb and Willsie to show up with that deed."

Broderick reached for one of Quarney's cigars, rolled it across his lips.

"Ever think that Clint may be playing some kind of come-on game, Mike? Maybe there isn't any deed. Maybe —."

"Now you're being thick-headed," cut in Quarney harshly. "Of course there's a deed. Where and why could Clint Brandon drag up his little idea if there wasn't a deed? I've done some checking. There was such a man as Quesada, and he did hole up somewhere down toward the river gap. No, young Brandon's offer stands up. But I'd see him in hell before I'd fork over fifteen thousand dollars. Not when I can get hold of that deed for nothing. Damn it all, why don't Korb and Willsie show up?"

Quarney pushed to his feet and began pacing the office.

Broderick watched him with narrowed eyes. Case Broderick had known Mike Quarney for quite a stretch of time, but only in the past year had he been really close to the man. Quarney had sought him out one day at Circle 60 and hinted of some development in the future that would make them both a lot of money, if Broderick was willing to work with him.

It had been a somewhat cautious approach toward a partnership, for each of them, ruthless in his own right, recognized a like strain in the other. There was another common ground on which they could meet — a hatred of Dan Brandon. With Broderick, that feeling came from an envy of what Brandon possessed and a deep-seated jealousy of the stature of the man and of the place he occupied on Big Sage

Prairie. For it was in Case Broderick to hate any man who threw a longer shadow than he did.

Mike Quarney's hatred of Brandon came from a more direct reason. Brandon had been the prime influence behind the voter revolt that had retired Mike Quarney to private life, and for that, Quarney had vowed eternal vengeance against Brandon, against the Brandon name, Brandon possessions, heirs and assigns, forever and forever.

Quarney's proposition had been that by joining forces they could both satisfy their hatred of Dan Brandon, and in the doing, amass wealth as well. In the end, agreement had been made. Quarney bought in on Circle 60 and since then they had worked steadily toward their common goal.

They had watched gloatingly the decline in Brandon's wellbeing. They had exulted at his death, foreseeing easy conquest after that. Then had come Martha Brandon's stunning disclosure that Leach Carlin was to take over and manage the affairs of Hackamore. This they had not remotely anticipated, but they had gone too far in their plans to turn away. The development that was to have given them their first big stride toward riches, the building of a dam in the river gap, was now an actuality in the near future. And with word of that, they had made their first move toward getting control of the Indian Mounds-Steptoe Creek range. That the move had more or less backfired in their faces had done nothing to shore up their confidence. Both had tried to convince themselves that Carlin's counter-move was no permanent obstacle, but both knew in their hearts that it shaped up otherwise.

Word of the deed that Hackamore held to the contested range had been another jolting surprise. And both knew that possession of the deed gave Hackamore a weapon that could smash their plan completely. And so Quarney had dealt with Clint and his unexpected offer. But in his own way, the way of one crook trying to outsmart another. And now they were on tenterhooks, awaiting the outcome of their scheming.

Quarney was showing the tension far more than Broderick, who now, as he watched Quarney pace up and down, measured this man's makeup as keenly as he could. Long ago Broderick had become quite sure of one thing. Quarney was primarily looking out for Quarney. He would use any man to his own advantage, discard him without the slightest concern.

Now, also, Broderick was measuring the true weight of Mike Quarney's courage. A hard man to read, Mike Quarney. That hatchet face, those thin, down-pulled lips, those bleak and shadowed eyes, rafty in their cold isolation, made up a mask it was difficult to see beyond. But events over the past day or two had torn aside some of that mask. Irascibility had shown through, and a shrill, almost shrewish temper that hinted at some inner uncertainty. Abruptly Broderick came to a decision. Here, he decided, was a good time and place to voice a thought that had been taking form over the past several weeks.

"Mike," he said abruptly, "I'm going to lay something on the line. Cutting it to a short, sweet pattern, here it is. Don't ever try and double-cross me! Don't even play with the thought. You do and I'll shoot your heart out!"

Quarney, his restless pacing having carried him to the far end of the room, came around as though hit by a blow. He rocked forward a little on his toes, staring at Broderick.

"What in hell kind of talk is that?" he rapped.

"Straight talk," shot back Broderick. "Since forming our little tie-in, you've gradually been taking on the attitude that you're the senior partner, and so, you've been throwing your weight around more than's been called for. Where some of our moves have slipped up a little, you've been a little too ready to throw the blame on everybody. else. You've thrown the rawhide into me. Well, that's all done with, Mike. I don't take it any more. Every move I've made has been, for the most part, a move that you agreed upon. So if it's turned up wrong, you're as much at fault as I am. No, there'll be no more rawhide thrown my way, and remember what I just said about a double-cross. I meant every word — every damn word!"

Their glances met, locked. It was Quarney's that first slid away.

"Where," he demanded, that shrill, shrewish note creeping into his voice, "did you ever get the impression that I was, as you put it, intending to double-cross you? That's ridiculous. You and I are partners in this thing. I need you and you need me. In all fairness, you should apologize for that thought, Case."

Broderick shrugged. "If I'm wrong, and time proves me wrong, I'll apologize. But if I'm right, then you're a dead man, Mike."

Quarney went fully behind his mask. Then he strode over to his desk, reached for the bottle of rye and poured two more drinks. His laugh was too thin to be convincing.

"Hell, Case, we're acting like children,

rather than grown men. Here's looking at you!"

Broderick downed his drink, said nothing more.

Quarney was lighting a fresh cigar when Duff Randall's heavy step sounded in the rear of the house. Coming into the room, Randall shook his head.

"No sign of Clint, or of Korb and Willsie either," he reported. "What do we do now?"

Mike Quarney, not answering, got to his feet and began pacing again. Broderick watched him for a moment, then turned his head and gave Randall an answer.

"Just wait it out right here, Duff."

They came in on Circle 60 headquarters from the east, following the looping run of the meadows along Antelope Creek. Leach Carlin, Hitch Wheeler, and Joe Spence rode in the lead and in silence.

Cattle stirred from bedding grounds and gave way in front of the steadily jogging horses. Night caught and muffled sound, the soft thump of hoofs on the spongy meadow ground, the creak of saddle leather, and the occasional faint tinkle of bit or spur chain. The fall season was in the chilling air and in the cold scintillating of the stars. Once, haunting in its wild loneliness, the call of geese, winging south, drifted down from among those same stars.

They picked up the lights of Circle 60 and Carlin reined in, letting the others move up until he felt himself surrounded by the panting horses and the warm, equine odor rising from them.

"I don't know what we'll find up there," said Carlin. "But Hitch and I are going in for a close look. Joe, you bring the other boys up to where Hitch and I leave our horses. Wait there."

Carlin and Hitch Wheeler moved on again, holding their mounts to a walk. Presently Hitch murmured. "Close enough with broncs. They could be smart enough to have guards out."

So they swung down, took their spurs off, and hung them on their saddle horns. They ground-reined the horses and prowled on afoot. What had been just pin points of yellow light now took on the squared form of windows. Against night's fullness the black outlines of buildings bulked. The main cabin was dark, the lights that showed coming from the windows of the bunkhouse.

Carlin and Wheeler stole cautiously closer. Hitch stopped, laid a hand on Carlin's arm. "Don't think they got any guards out," he murmured. "But I want to make sure. Wait here, Leach."

Hitch was just a gaunt shadow, slipping off into the dark. Carlin waited, turning his intentions in this thing over in his mind. There would, he told himself, be no halfway measures. There would be no arbitration, no truce, no promise of a peace that would never be a true peace. Circle 60 had thrown down the gage. Circle 60 had killed — first. This thing must be absolute!

Hitch Wheeler came as he had gone, shadow silent. "No guards," he reported softly. "Main cabin is empty. Everybody that's here is in the bunkhouse. Want me to bring up the other boys?"

"Go get 'em," Carlin answered.

Left alone, Carlin moved in on the bunkhouse. He stopped short of the reach of the light from the windows. He saw a figure pass one window and recognized Ward Dancy. A little later the heavier bulk of Frank Labine shouldered by the same lighted area. A twist of night air brought the tang of wood smoke to Carlin's nostrils. They had a fire going in there, against night's chill.

The faint stir of movement behind Carlin told him of the arrival of Hitch and the balance of the Hackamore crew. Carlin led them around to the bunkhouse door. With his left hand he felt for and located the latch of the door, with his right he drew his gun. He pulled the latch, swung the door wide and stepped through.

"Don't anybody move!"

Only four men were there in the bunk-house. Frank Labine, Ward Dancy, Shep Bowen, and Vern DeLong. Dancy was seated at the table, a half-dealt hand of solitaire in front of him. Labine and Bowen were lounging on their bunks. DeLong was in his, his face drawn and full of a sick pallor under its swarthiness. His blankets were not pulled high enough to cover a shoulder heavily swathed in a pad of white bandage.

Carlin's order had its full effect on three of them, who froze exactly as they were. De-Long rolled his head, half lifted it and his black, fever-burned eyes flared with a red, but helpless hate.

Carlin moved deeper into the bunkhouse, with Wheeler and Joe Spence and the rest crowding in behind him. Carlin said, "First, get their guns!"

Wheeler and Spence took care of this. Vern DeLong's was hanging on a wall peg above his bunk and as Wheeler reached and lifted it down, DeLong sent words up at him, blurred and guttural.

"I'll spend the rest of my life wishing you

in hell, Wheeler. For wrecking my shoulder, damn you!"

Hitch looked down at him with no show of rancor. "You picked the wrong horse to ride, Vern. A man makes his own luck, that way. Yours turned up bad."

There was no vestige of fight in any of the other three. Carlin looked them over, finally centering his glance on Ward Dancy. "Where's Broderick and Randall?"

Dancy was a weak reed, always had been. "Not here," he gulped.

"Hell, I can see that. Where are they? Don't try and stall on me, I'm in no mood for it. Where are they?"

"Town," answered Dancy. "Went in before dark."

"When will they be back?"

Dancy shrugged. "They didn't say."

Carlin was thoughtful for a moment, then let his glance run over the four of them again. "Just in case you're wondering," he said harshly, "I'll explain. This evening, out along the Hackamore town trail, Clint was killed. By Korb and Willsie. And —," he slowed his words for emphasis, "Korb and Willsie are dead, too."

Frank Labine reared half up on his bunk. Ward Dancy's chin wobbled and dropped. Shep Bowen drew a deep breath, then let it out in a faint sibilant hiss. Vern DeLong lay quite still, but his black eyes veiled with a sort of sullen hopelessness. Dancy got control of his chin and mumbled halting words.

"I — we — none of us had anything to do with that, Carlin. We've been right here at headquarters all day. We had nothing to do with that."

"If I thought you did," growled Carlin, "you'd all of you live just long enough to get to the nearest tree. But like Hitch told DeLong, you've made your choice of horses to ride. You've picked the wrong one and no fault but your own. So here is how it will be. You'll stay right here until morning, with Joe and the rest of the boys to keep an eye on you. Come tomorrow, the three of you who are able to, will fork your kaks and ride — across the mountains. You'll stay gone. If you ever show again on Big Sage Prairie, you'll be buried here.

"DeLong, you'll be moved to a hotel room, in town. And when you're able to, then you'll make the long ride, over the mountains. Circle 60 is going out of business — completely and for good. Broderick had full warning not to start something he couldn't stop."

He turned to Joe Spence. "Hitch and me

are heading for town, Joe. We're going looking for Broderick and Randall. If we miss on that and they show here, gather them in. If they try and make a fight of it you know what to do."

"Won't need all of us to keep these four in line," said Joe. "Better let me go along with you and Hitch."

Carlin shook his head. "You'll do, right here. Like I said, we may miss Broderick and Randall along the trail."

CHAPTER TWELVE

It had been a long night for Mike Quarney and Case Broderick. They had waited the slow hours out, and still no word from Korb and Willsie. They had sent Duff Randall on another prowl of town and Randall had returned with the same word as before. No sign anywhere of Clint Brandon, or of Korb and Willsie. Quarney had another of his shrill outbursts.

"They've run out on us, Korb and Willsie have. Damn them, we shouldn't have —."

"Run out where?" broke in Broderick. "And for what reason? Even if they knew what that deed meant, which they don't, what would they do with it? What could they do with it? Use your head, Quarney. Korb and Willsie didn't agree to this trick just for the hell of it. They went out to get that deed on the promise of extra money, and that's all they're interested in. So, they didn't run out on us. Something has happened that we didn't figure right."

Randall offered his opinion. "I could have told you it would. In bucking Hackamore, we're bucking Leach Carlin, and the luck of the devil rides with that man. I tell you I had him dead in my sights, that day below the Indian Mounds. And just as I touched off the shot, he swung his horse. Then that other hombre bought in, from somewhere behind me, so I couldn't get another try."

"Let it lay, Duff," growled Broderick. "You missed him, that's all. You just plain as hell missed him."

Randall subsided into surly silence. Broderick turned to Quarney. "Sit down, Mike, and quit that damned pacing. What's the matter — your guts running out?"

Quarney gave Broderick a savage stare, but he resumed his chair. He chewed his cigar for a time in silence, then said, "What are we going to do about it?"

The mirthless smile that curled Case Broderick's lips held a shadow of contempt in it.

"Running out of ideas, too, eh, Mike? Well, I'm not. I'm going to start giving orders now. Here's what we're going to do. We're staying right here for the rest of the night. Come morning, Duff and I will get out and around and shake up some answers. Let's see that bottle — and another glass this time. Duff is in on this drink. I know where Duff stands, but I'm beginning to wonder about you."

A thin stain of anger ran across Quarney's gaunt cheeks, but he said nothing more.

After midnight, warmed by two or three drinks, Randall went to sleep, hunkered down against the wall, head settled on his chest. Broderick slid low in his chair, hat pulled far over his eyes. He gave the appearance of being asleep himself, but through slitted eyes he was watching Mike Quarney and several times caught the cold glint of Quarney's gaze, studying him.

In the black morning hours, Quarney stirred in his chair and pushed stiffly to his feet. Broderick's voice bit at him.

"Where you going, Mike?"

"To cook a pot of coffee," came the snapping answer.

Broderick said, "Good! I'll go along."

Quarney carried the lamp to the kitchen, got a fire going in the stove, cooked up the coffee. The stir of movement and the smell of coffee aroused Randall and he came into the kitchen, too, blinking heavy lids.

The coffee helped. It warmed and stimulated, brought a measure of relaxation from the long tension of the night. They emptied the pot while watching dawn light begin to pale beyond the kitchen windows.

"Better," said Quarney, almost heartily.

"Daylight's where a man should live. Night always is a bad time for me."

Broderick looked at him cynically. "Don't tell me you have a conscience, Mike, and the dark sets it to working overtime?"

Again that thin stain of angry color touched Quarney's hatchet face, and again he kept his silence.

It had been a long night for Leach Carlin and Hitch Wheeler, too. It was just short of midnight when they rode into Modoc City, and the town had folded up for the night. The only light showing was in the Skyhigh and when they left their horses and turned in here, Ace Lanier was alone and about to close up. Ace pushed out bottle and glass and grunted wearily.

"Looks like it's one of those nights. The regular stud game didn't break up until near an hour later than usual. These late hours are making an old man out of me." Then, seeing that this heavy attempt at humor brought no break in the settled sternness of Carlin's expression, Ace added, "What's wrong, Leach — something happened I don't know about?"

Carlin pouring drinks for Hitch and himself, nodded soberly. "Clint's dead," he said quietly. "A couple of strange hard-case riders of Broderick's killed him."

Ace stared, then swore softly. "And you're looking for them?"

"No, not them. They've already been taken care of. Hitch and me, we're looking for Broderick and Duff Randall. They been around?"

"Ain't seen nothing of Broderick," informed Ace. "But a couple of times Randall showed. Stuck his head in here twice, earlier in the evening, like he might have been looking for somebody. That's all he did do — just stuck his head in, looked the place over, then went on his way."

Carlin nodded slowly, as though this item of information fitted in with some previous conviction he'd arrived at. Ace, still blinking over what Carlin had told him, asked, "How'd it happen — about Clint, I mean?"

Carlin tossed off his drink then evaded direct answer. "Put it that Circle 60 has broke over the final edge, Ace. Come on, Hitch."

The doors winnowed shut behind them. Ace got out another glass, poured a short one for himself and ruminated a moment over it. Unable to locate any definite answer, he shook his head and began putting out the lights.

"Fireworks ahead," he muttered. "Carlin's

got the same look about him that he had the day he took Randall apart in here."

Carlin and Wheeler prowled the dark and silent town from end to end. Aside from their own, not horse was at any of the hitch rails. The door of Pee Dee Kyne's hotel was closed, but not locked; and Carlin tiptoed in, scratched a match, and looked over the register. Outside again he told Hitch, "If they turned in for the night here, they never signed up."

They went down to Coony Fyle's livery and prowled all through there, murmuring softly to calm the stabled horses, using matches to survey brands. Not a Circle 60 iron showed. Outside again, looking up and down, Carlin twisted up a smoke and spoke somberly.

"We must have missed them along the trail, Hitch. They're not in town."

"Not too sure of that," said Hitch briefly. "One place we haven't looked, yet. Mike Quarney's house."

Carlin made a disgusted gesture. "I'm growing lunk-headed. Come on!"

They went south along the street, turned off it, and worked a careful way up to the Quarney house. It looked just as dark and still as the rest of the town, but when Carlin and Hitch circled it cautiously they saw just the faintest line of light past the edge of a drawn shade.

"That's Quarney's office," said Hitch softly. "Somebody's in there."

They circled to the back of the place and stopped abruptly. A horse gave a gusty sigh, stamped a hoof. They moved with the greatest care, investigating. Two horses were there. Carlin drew Hitch back a little.

"We didn't miss them after all," he murmured. "They're in there with Quarney. Waiting. Waiting for somebody who'll never show. Korb and Willsie. This ties everything in, Hitch."

Hitch hooked his thumbs in his gunbelt, stared at the dark bulk of the house. "Shall we go in after them?"

Carlin considered, then shook his head. "Not yet. I don't want any slip-up now. We couldn't get in without them hearing us, for they're sure to be listening — for Korb and Willsie. And while the dark has advantages in some cases, it has drawbacks, too. It could help them in a getaway. One thing is sure, Broderick and Randall won't leave without their horses. So, we'll wait it out and watch, right here!"

It was a long, cold wait. The dark pressed in, thick and chilling, and time moved with dragging slowness. Along the years of solitary trails he had traveled, Hitch Wheeler had learned the locked-in, stoic patience of an Indian. He had the knack of pushing time away from him, letting it flow past without impact.

With Leach Carlin, this waiting was a tougher chore. His emotions urged him to smash right into the house, force the show-down, get it over with. But his common sense told him otherwise, and ruled the moment. He wanted no slip-up, no chance at leaving the job unfinished. So he waited.

Time, he found, however slow it could seem at times, did move. And dawn, when it came, arrived with startling suddenness. Night's blackness was fading to a filtering gray, out of which the solid things of the world began to emerge with ever-sharpening outline.

Abruptly there was the glow of lamplight in a rear window of the house. Then a whiff of wood smoke filtering down through dawn's moist air. Hitch tipped his head.

"They'll be able to see us here if they should happen to take a look," he whispered. "If you're going to wait longer, we better get past the corner of the house."

They did this. Carlin automatically began to build a smoke, realized abruptly that this wouldn't do, rumpled the paper and let the pinch of tobacco filter from his fingers.

Streaks of silver and rose lancing up from behind the far Nevada Hills, and a lifting light over the whole world. Full dawn, now, dawn running into morning when men awoke to the measure of another day. Birds stirring in the poplars, then winging high for a first glimpse of the sun.

The back door of Mike Quarney's house opened and Broderick and Randall stepped out. Quarney's gaunt figure filled the doorway and Broderick turned to him for a final word.

"I'll get word to you just as soon as Duff and I find out what's happened. If Korb and Willsie should show, keep them here until I get back. All right, Duff, let's go!"

Leach Carlin and Hitch Wheeler stepped into view past the corner of the house.

"Go where, Broderick?"

It held Broderick and Randall, frozen still. In the doorway, Mike Quarney made a funny sound in his throat, but that was all. In a chill, implacable way, Carlin went on.

"You needn't look for Korb and Willsie, and don't wait for them. They'll never show — because they're dead. They killed Clint, and now they're dead. Broderick, the trail's run out. Now it's you!"

Case Broderick knew that. He knew it the

moment he looked at Carlin. He read it in the set of this big man's bitterly grim mouth and jaw, in the cold menace of his eyes. The words Carlin was speaking were outer things, sounds at the edge of Broderick's consciousness. The import of them registered like vague echoes. Korb and Willsie dead! And now —

Broderick set himself by shifting one foot slightly. The move was a tip-off; Carlin spotted it, and he was drawing as Broderick drew.

Carlin did not hear the sound of his shot, nor feel the leaping recoil of the heavy gun, jarring back against his palm. He was lost in his concentration on his target — the center of Case Broderick's chest.

He saw the light flutter of Broderick's shirt where the bullet hit; he saw the smash of the slug lift Broderick, shake him; he saw Broderick's knees buckle and let him down. And he saw the gout of earth leap up in front of him where Broderick's bullet gouged, too late, too wild.

The belting echoes seemed to drive Mike Quarney away from the door, and Duff Randall, with surprising quickness for all his heavy-bodied thickness, leaped for the same sanctuary, just ahead of Hitch Wheeler's bullet, that would have taken Randall center had he not moved, but now was only a scratch burn across Randall's ribs. Hitch swore thinly and darted for the door himself. He beat Carlin there by two long strides.

Duff Randall's mind was a turmoil, a wild jumble. He'd heard the bullet hit Broderick, heard Broderick's mortal gasp, and knew that he was dead. Case Broderick, the one man in Duff Randall's life ever to win his complete fidelity. In Randall's eyes, Broderick had been a man to follow with dog-like devotion. Broderick had been the big prop in his life, the anchor of all his thinking and his actions. Now he was dead, and the knowledge was dread thunder in Randall's brain. It loomed above all realization of his own position. Rage and a strange, blind grief had Duff Randall by the throat and he went shooting crazy.

Ahead of him was Mike Quarney running along the shadowy hall toward the front of the house. And abruptly, in that gaunt, dark figure, Duff Randall felt that he saw the real cause of Broderick's death. Quarney had sucked Case Broderick into his schemes, used him and left him lying dead and now was trying for a run-out —.

Randall pushed his gun level and the roar of it was a trapped, flat rumble. Unseen force hammered between Mike Quarney's shoulders, knocking him forward and down in a long, sliding sprawl. Randall half stumbled over the man he'd just killed, slammed into the front door of the house, fumbled at the key, at the knob.

Then Hitch Wheeler's thin and deadly challenge came along the hall.

"Randall — !"

Randall came around, feet spread, a crouched, heavy figure. His lips were flattened in a snarl and a strange, guttural growl was an eruptive sound in his throat. Wheeler's first slug took him just above the belt buckle.

Randall's growl became a moan. He threw his gun again and again, wildly, blindly — for he couldn't see, he couldn't feel, now. Couldn't feel the lead that cut into him twice more; everything was falling away.

The last echoes clubbed their way about the house, thinned to nothingness. Leach Carlin, coming into the hallway, found Hitch standing over Mike Quarney's sprawled, still figure.

"Randall," said Hitch, in a quiet, faraway tone. "Randall did it. And I got Randall."

Carlin went quietly out, waited. Shortly Hitch appeared. A strange calm was on him, and he spoke the same way.

"A man's life," said Hitch, "can fall into

two parts. One part of mine is closed — for good. The other — I look forward to." Then, more softly, he added, "He picked his own trail to ride. It wasn't the right one. And it's run out."

Men were gathering, drawn by the muffled pound of guns. Billy Prior, Coony Fyle, Doc Persall — then Ace Lanier and Lyle Barnard and others.

Quietly, grave of face, Leach Carlin told them how it was. He told them about Clint and about those two riders of Broderick's, Korb and Willsie. The only thing he didn't tell was Clint's trickery with the Quesada deed. They listened, sober and subdued, mature men who had seen something like this shaping up since Dan Brandon's passing. Now they rendered judgment, and it was fair. Billy Prior spoke for all of them.

"They started the fire — and got caught in the middle of it."

Doc Persall, as coroner, took over. Lyle Barnard pulled Leach aside.

"Right now," the banker said, "it is probably of much less concern to you, Leach. But I got an answer to one of my letters. It came as a telegram over the railroad wire to Centerville. Swing Benson brought it to me. The authority for a dam on Big Sage River has been passed, and the money appropriated for it. Brandon's twenty-five hundred dollar gamble is going to pay off big!"

Carlin listened, almost absently. "Thanks for all your trouble, Lyle," he said presently. "Only, there's one change to make. It's cost a lot more than twenty-five hundred."

CHAPTER THIRTEEN

It lacked half an hour of midday when Carlin came up to headquarters. Weariness, more of the spirit than physical, was a weight on his shoulders, and a gray reluctance rode doggedly at his elbow. The happenings of the past twenty-four hours had been enough to leave any man drained and somber, but Carlin would gladly have lived the savage hours over again a dozen times, rather than face what now lay ahead of him. Yet, it had to be done. Martha Brandon had to be told.

He took his time about unsaddling and corraling his horse. He built a cigarette and found it tasteless and of no comfort. Violence, he mused darkly, could take everything out of a man, leaving him with no normal reactions at all. Standing by the corral gate he took a long look around and in the near distance saw a faint haze of dust lifting. That, he concluded, would be a buckboard coming. Bois Renfro was being good to his word. Nora and Dallas Renfro would be in the buckboard, bringing their understanding and comfort for Martha to lean upon.

He dropped his cigarette, ground it under a boot, squared his shoulders and crossed to the ranch house. He let himself in at the side office door and paused beside the desk, trying to frame an approach that would give Martha the word in as gentle a way as possible.

But, how could a man soften a thing of this sort — ?

He heard her step in the hall beyond the inner door. Then the door swung open and she came in, erect, snowy-haired, half smiling, half grave.

"I was hoping you'd show, Leach. Last night was a very long one, with everybody away from the ranch. It's given me the feeling that things have been happening and of course I want to know about them. I've wondered —"

The quiet, even run of her voice broke and stilled. For now, as she moved deeper into the room and Carlin turned to face her, the light of the windows struck him more fully and what she saw in the settled gravity of his features and the somber shadow in his eyes made her catch her breath and drew a paleness across her cheeks.

"Leach! What is it? Something — what — ?"

There was, he realized now, no way that

a thing of this sort could be eased. The facts were dominant and overrode everything else. And the quick way would be the more merciful way, after all.

"It's Clint," said Carlin. "He's gone, Mrs. Brandon."

"Gone! You mean — ?" She put a hand on the corner of the desk as though to steady herself, and her voice dropped to little more than a strained whisper. "You don't mean that Clint is dead?"

Carlin nodded. "Yes."

She swayed a little and Carlin was quickly beside her, offering the support of his arm. She leaned against him for a moment and Carlin, with a hooking boot toe, dragged the desk chair around so that she could sink into it.

She sat there, crumpled and shaken and still, staring straight ahead at nothing. Carlin waited, not knowing what to do or what further to say. A long half minute dragged by, seconds surcharged with the helplessness all men and women must know before the inexorability of a thing of this sort.

Then Martha Brandon's snowy head lifted, her shoulders straightened and her voice came, quiet and strong again.

"Tell me, Leach."

Carlin cleared his throat. "A pair of Circle

60 riders did it. By name; Korb and Willsie. Two strangers, hard cases that Broderick brought in. They met up with Clint between here and town last evening. There was an argument of some sort. They shot him. Hitch Wheeler and I happened along just as it took place, though too late to stop it. But," and here his voice harshened, "not too late to even up. We took care of Korb and Willsie. That — that's it, Mrs. Brandon."

"But why — why?" she cried softly. "Did Broderick order it? Has the man gone completely mad? What could he hope to gain by — by — ?"

"Broderick is all through gaining anything, Mrs. Brandon. That goes for Mike Quarney, too. They'll never bother Hackamore or any of its parts again."

She looked up at him, her eyes wet, but her face strangely quiet. "What do you mean, Leach? Did you — ?"

Carlin nodded, took a short turn up and down the room. Harshness roughened his tone again.

"They started it — they forced the whole thing. You recall that day in the hotel, the day you asked me to take over at Hackamore, the day Broderick came in and laid his cards on the table about the Indian Mounds-Steptoe Creek range? Well, I told

302

him then that if he started real trouble he'd choke on it. So — after Clint — Hitch Wheeler and I called on Mister Broderick and Mister Quarney. Duff Randall was there, too. Now it's finshed!"

He paused by a window, staring out. Martha watched him. She needed to be told no more. Case Broderick and Mike Quarney were dead. One way or another, this big man at the window had seen to that. They had gone to the gun and he had finished it with a gun.

A tough man to fill a tough saddle — that was what she had asked for. That was what she had got. It was what Hackamore had needed, what Hackamore had to have. And that tough saddle — how Leach Carlin had filled it — !

Somehow she knew he was waiting for her judgment. She got up and walked over beside him, put her hand on his arm.

"You did only what you had to do, Leach. I know that. You were the kind of man I asked you to be. But why did Clint — have to be what he was? I'm remembering him now as he was as a baby —"

Here the tears really came and Carlin put an arm around her.

Outside, a buckboard rolled up. Dallas Renfro and her mother were in it. They got down and came straight to the office door. Carlin called them in.

Two weeks had passed. Again things were moving at the old pace at Hackamore. Life, mused Leach Carlin, was like that. Man-made storms roared to a peak, exhausted their fury, and frittered out. And life went on, for those lucky enough to have survived the storm.

The crew was at work, readying all the multitude of ranch affairs in preparation for the winter soon to come. Cattle had to be moved from more exposed range to a more sheltered one. Barns, feed sheds, buildings of all kinds had to be gone over and made secure. Man's destiny was to work, and it was a good destiny.

Carlin had stayed away from the ranch house as much as he could. But this day there were affairs in the office to take care of. So he was in there when Martha Brandon came in.

"I want," she said, "to speak to you about Clint again, Leach. Just this one more time. Those two, Korb and Willsie, must have had more than a casual reason for — for what they did. I've a feeling that you didn't tell me all the story, Leach — and I want it all. Don't worry about my feelings. Remember our promise, Leach — no evasion, no secrets."

Carlin saw that this white-haired woman would never be satisfied with anything less than the truth, so he told her all of it. When he finished, she nodded slowly, gravely.

"I had a feeling that it was something like that. My estimate of Clint was right. He just couldn't be true."

She moved to a window, stood looking out across a world that again knew peace. She said, without turning, "But you'll be true, Leach — true to Hackamore and all the good things it stands for. And that makes me very happy. Because, you know, one day Hackamore will be yours, Leach."

He blinked, not sure that he had heard right. "Mrs. Brandon — what was that you said?"

She came around, met his glance and nodded. "All yours, some day, Leach. My will to that effect is in one of Lyle Barnard's strong boxes. It is the way I wish it. There is no one else. And you are like Dan was, far back when he and I were young. A man big enough to fill a tough saddle, and strong enough to ride it. In your hands, Hackamore will always be safe."

Outside, a buckboard rattled up. Driving it was Dallas Renfro and with her was her mother. Martha Brandon, a shine of gladness in her eyes, hurried to the main ranch-house door to let them in. Listening, Carlin could hear the murmur of their voices, and knew a swift warmth. How good a thing real friendship could be, friendship to comfort a gallant woman now grown old and lonely.

And the friendship between men, too. Carlin thought of Hitch Wheeler, out somewhere riding with the rest of the Hackamore crew. No longer a lonely outcast, but one of them. Happy and contented with, as he had put it, the second half of his life.

The office's inner door opened and Dallas Renfro came in. As she found a chair she gave Carlin a long, sober look.

"Not a thing new about me," jibed Carlin. "The same heavy-footed hombre as always."

"You sure, Leach?" she asked.

She was, he thought, the fairest thing his eyes had ever rested on. He got up and went over and stood beside her.

"Stand up," he ordered. "I want you closer to me, so you'll mistake nothing I say to you."

When she did not immediately obey, he bent, scooped her slenderness up in both arms and cradled her easily, despite her best wrigglings and struggles.

"Leach Carlin, you put me down. Let go of me!"

He smiled into a pair of gray eyes, so faultless and so soft as to give the complete lie to her voiced objections.

"Not now," he told her. "Not now — or ever, Dallas. Understand, not ever!"

Her voice shook a little. "If I could only believe him — if I could only believe him!"

"Look at me," he told her. "Look at me — good!"

She did, no longer struggling. Her smile was a gentle, dawning glory. Simply, she said, "I believe, Leach."

Then her arms were around his neck and her lips a reaching sweetness.

The office door opened and Nora Renfro exclaimed, "Sakes alive! Such goings on!"

At Nora Renfro's side, Martha Brandon smiled mistily. "It is what I've hoped for," she said.

L.P. Holmes was the author of a number of outstanding Western novels. Born in a snowed-in log cabin in the heart of the Rockies near Breckenridge, Colorado in 1895, Holmes moved with his family when very young to northern California and it was here that his father and older brothers built the ranch house where Holmes grew up and where, in later life, he would live again. He published his first story — "The Passing of the Ghost" — in ACTION STORIES (9/25). He was paid ½¢ a word and received a check for $40. "Yeah — forty bucks," he said later. "Don't laugh. In those far-off days . . . a pair of young parents with a three-year-old son could buy a lot of groceries on forty bucks." He went on to contribute nearly 600 stories of varying lengths to the magazine market as well as to write over fifty Western novels under his own name and the byline Matt Stuart. For many years of his life, Holmes would write in the mornings and spend his afternoons calling on a group of friends in town, among them the blind Western author Charles H. Snow whom Lew Holmes always called "Judge" Snow (because he was Napa's Justice of the

Peace (1920–1924) and who frequently makes an appearance in later novels as a local justice in Holmes's imaginary Western communities. Holmes's Golden Age as an author was from 1948 through 1960. During these years he produced such notable novels as DESERT RAILS, BLACK SAGE, SUMMER RANGE, DEAD MAN'S SADDLE, and SOMEWHERE THEY DIE for which he received the Golden Spur Award from the Western Writers of America. In these novels one finds the themes so basic to his Western fiction: the loyalty which unites one man to another, the pride one must take in his work and a job well done, the innate generosity of most of the people who live in Holmes's ambient Western communities, and the vital relationship between a man and a woman in making a better life.